Advance Praise for

"Deceptively simple and beautifully ill
fully illustrates the magic of healing relationships. This engaging story
follows a group of irascible dragons - the kind most people give up on as
hopelessly irredeemable - and their novice camp counselor, Max, through
their adventures at dragon camp. As each dragon faces his or her personal
challenges under the caring and perceptive eyes of the camp's hosts, suspi-
cion and hostility give way to self compassion and hope.

Wisdom, glittering like gemstones strewn throughout the story,
draws on deep understandings derived from both sides of the healing
relationship. On the way to finding validation and acceptance of their
deep-seated feelings of anger, grief, and alienated loneliness, the youth-
ful dragons learn that 'mistakes are how we learn' and that anything is
possible when we truly believe in ourselves. Their transformation from
delinquents to dragons deserving of second chances and fresh starts
builds on a deep belief in their potential conveyed by teachers who,
importantly, 'see through the fault to the need.' *Dragon Camp* carries
a message of hope to young people in deep need of help, and to those
who would seek to help them."

   -Nancy Vanderheide, Ph.D., Psychoanalyst and Author

"Curl up with a steaming mug of dragon berry tea and enjoy *Dragon
Camp*. This tale is for all dragons --young and young at heart —who
need to know that someone understands their struggles to find their
place in the world.

Drawing on her extensive experience working with troubled children,
Cate Shepherd creates characters that many readers can connect with.

Join Max, Raif and the rest of the campers as they learn how to embrace their talents and help each other develop the skills to succeed.

   - Ely Rareshide, Author

"In the therapeutic environment of Dragon Camp, where person-
ality quirks and artistic expression are valued, dragon spirits soar and
deep friendships bloom. Parallel storylines build at a satisfying pace,
and Dr. Shepherd deftly juggles them all to a satisfying conclusion.

Colorful illustrations bring the story vividly alive. Young readers will
find much to interest them --including distinctive characters, romance,
boxing, martial arts, skateboarding, and hints of magic."

   -Scott Barbour, Author & Editor

Advance Praise for Dragon Camp

"Cate Shepherd, as usual, writes with great heart. Her novel, Dragon Camp about a group of delinquent and semi-delinquent juvenile dragons at summer camp made me feel as if I were being warmly embraced even while its campers got into all sorts of trouble, whether because they were pitching food fights, throwing punches, lighting fires, or going AWOL.

Cate offers the readers, along with the dragons, methods to master their "lizard brains" through such devices as dragonmeters and STAR, (you'll have to read the novel to find out what this means!). She also offers up humor, lots of it, some of it subtle, some not so much. For example, consider the names of the adult humans at the summer camp: Mrs. Cleerheart, Mrs. Sear, and Mr. Yuni. And the artwork by Doug Jennings burns and sizzles with originality.

So, make yourself some Drowsy Dragon tea, sit down and take a stroll through Dragon Camp."

-Suad Campell, Author

"Imagine you're a troubled, young dragon who finds that life is always rubbing your scales the wrong way. Perhaps you're a small, pink dragon who's shy, or big, red dragon who finds it difficult to control your fire-breathing anger. Where might you turn for help? The answer, of course, is Dragon Camp. Cate Shepherd's imaginative story is chock-full of relatable teen-aged dragons facing personal dilemmas. With help from the human and dragon camp counselors, the young dragons learn to overcome their problems and discover keys to growth and hope. Following the adventures of this group of amusing and mischievous dragons, the reader may just pick up a hint on how to improve his or her own life. Come join the fun at Dragon Camp. There be dragons here. What more could you want?

P.S. Doug Jennings' illustrations are wonderful.

-John Edward Mullen, award-winning author of *Digital Dick*

DRAGON CAMP

See extra art and behind-scene-stories online at:
dragoncamp.info

Cover/book design by O. Douglas Jennings

First Edition December 2016

Dedication from Cate:

For all the precious children, parents, and teachers who inspired this story. And for dragons of all ages who light up our lives with their intensity, sensitivity, and brilliance.

Dedication from Doug:

To my wonderful daughters, Emily & Melody. You are miraculous blessings in my life. You both have inspired me as I've worked on Dragon Camp and have taught me so much about being a parent and a human being.

Acknowledgements

This book is the outcome of a spontaneous collaboration between two college friends who became reacquainted after many years and over many miles. It's been fun to catch up, and to inspire each other with our passions for helping families, writing, and making art. We're so grateful for the opportunity to make Dragon Camp a reality, and for the delightful creative process that brought us here.

- **Doug and Cate**

I thank my wife, Shanaz, for her love and support (It's not easy for a scientist to be married to an artist!) as well as input, encouragement and advice on early drafts of *Dragon Camp* from my sister, librarian Alicia Tippins, and fellow Art Instructor Alayne McNulty and fellow Art student Kathy Moseler.

- **O. Douglas Jennings, December 2016**

I want to thank my writing buddies and mentors who provided support and coaching along the way. Special thanks to Scott and Suad for your generous encouragement and critique. And to Jean Jenkins, a great editor and teacher. And, of course, all of the children and families who inspired the baby dragon concept and helped bring it to life.

And big thanks to my old friend, Doug Jennings for his tireless, joyful work on the book, the blog, and the videos. For his generosity and friendship. And for sending me those four adorable baby dragons who started this whole thing.

- **Cate Shepherd, December, 2016**

Dragon Camp
Chapter One

Slam! Clank!

Raif's cell went pitch black as the last guard locked the detention door and clomped away down a long, musty hall toward the front gate.

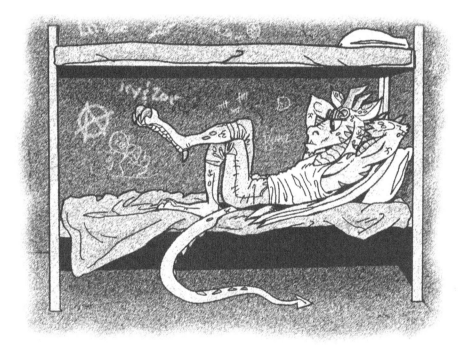

Bedtime was the worst part of the day to be an orphan in jail. No one to talk to, no one to write to, and no one to even think about. Sometimes it felt like sinking into a dark sea.

Raif pulled his tattered t-shirt off over his horns, wrapped it around a stick, and breathed a blast of flames to make a torch.

Tonight was cold, and he wished he had a lot more things to burn.

He scooted his paw across the dirt floor and found a sharp rock to chisel his initials into the cell wall.

As the torch burned down, black smoke flooded Raif's cell and tickled his nostrils. A flaming sneeze exploded from his snout. Then another one. Then another.

The fire alarm clanged.

A stampede of boots tromped toward his cell. Keys clattered against metal bars.

"All right, that's it." A gruff guard with a club grabbed Raif's wing and dragged him out into the hall.

Raif yelped in pain, jerked free, and glared at the guard. Smoke streamed from his hot nostrils.

"This time you're going down, dragon." He shoved Raif into two other guards who cuffed and shackled him. "No more second chances. Take him to long-term before he burns this place down."

Raif struggled and kicked as the guards dragged him down the dark hallway.

He wanted to roast both of them to a crackly crunch, but then it would be the dungeon instead of long-term detention.

And dragons who went to the dungeon never came back.

Chapter Two

Max stared into the flames of a late night campfire. An orchestra of crickets echoed across the lake, and fireflies danced around the edge of the forest. The sweet fragrance of night blooming jasmine made his snout itch.

Mr. Yuni, director of Dragon Camp, sat next to Max on a creaky, wooden bench. He had been training Max all week. Five disturbed dragons would arrive in the morning, and Max was their new counselor.

Max poked at the fire with a scorchbark branch. His tail flicked.

"We have some impulsive pups this summer." Mr. Yuni furrowed his forehead till his salt and pepper eyebrows met in the middle. "With these drought conditions we can't tolerate any fire-breathing."

Startled, Max looked over at his new mentor with wide green eyes full of guilt. Twelve years had passed since he accidentally set his classroom on fire, but that still wasn't enough distance. Max wished he could erase that shameful secret from his memory.

Max's teacher hadn't mentioned the classroom fire when she recommended him for the camp counselor job. She said he deserved a fresh start and besides, that was a long time ago.

"One of the older males is coming straight from detention." Mr. Yuni's voice snapped Max back into the present moment. "His probation officer called this morning and asked us to give him one last chance before he goes to long-term."

"How did he get into detention?" Max crinkled his forehead scales.

"Fighting, fire-breathing..."

Max gulped.

"He doesn't like authority figures."

Max cringed at the thought of being singed. "He must have a lot of anger."

Mr. Yuni nodded.

Chapter Three: First Day of Camp

The next morning, Max heard strange sounds from the dining hall and scurried across camp to check it out.

"Eww!" A chubby, orange dragon with sparkly green eyes hurled a big paw full of pink goop across the dining hall at a stocky blue dragon.

Splat! The blob landed on his head and ran down his cheek. "Hey!" He wiped his scales with the back of his paw.

It was Sammie and Nate, already embroiled in a food fight, and covered in fish pie. Sammie bolted around the dining hall in a victory lap. "I won! I won!"

Molly, a shy dragon, hovered near the doorway clutching her arms against her chest. She scrunched up her snout at the noisy battle of pie. The mess made her eyebrow scales twitch.

In the far corner, a lanky purple dragon named Phil leaned against the wall and gazed at Molly. When she spotted him, his face turned bright red.

"Hey, guys. Let's settle down." Counselor Max stood in the doorway with his paws propped on his hips. "Sammie and Nate, please clean up your mess."

Nate laughed. He scooped some pie off of his head and licked his finger. "Mmm!"

Phil slipped out the back door unnoticed during the commotion.

Max shook his head, strode out of the dining hall, and squinted into the bright morning sun. Tires crunched on the gravel, and he turned to watch a young adult dragon climb out of a truck that said Detention on the side. Metal piercings jutted out from the delinquent's eyebrow scales, and a pterodactyl tattoo curved over one of his muscular shoulders. His blue eyes darted from side to side.

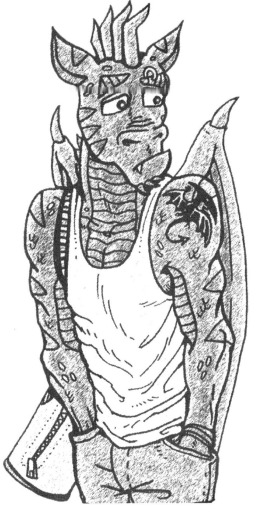

"You must be Raif." Max took a step toward him, smiled, and extended a paw. "I'm Max."

Raif's eyes went cold and his lip curled in a snarl. He looked Max up and down but said nothing.

Raif's probation officer quickly stepped up and shook Max's paw. "Thank you so much for giving Raif this opportunity." He gave Max an earnest look. "This is his last chance to avoid adult detention. I hope he'll make the most of it."

Max looked at Raif. "I'm sure you'll do well."

Raif rolled his eyes.

The P.O. gripped Raif's shoulder. "It's up to you now, son."

Raif looked down and clawed at the dirt.

The P.O. looked at Max. "Thank you. I'll be in touch."

Raif turned and watched him drive away.

Chapter Four

Max's first day as camp counselor felt a lot like herding jungle cats. He was responsible for keeping five dragons on task as they moved from orientation to lunch to cleanup then quiet time and on to Mr. Yuni's yoga class. Then from yoga to rec to showers to dinner to cleanup to evening meditation and to bed.

But Phil kept disappearing. And Raif took advantage of the first day's chaos to explore the woods.

The emotional pull of Molly's bed made it impossible for her to participate. She had a headache, a stomachache, a sore foot, and a feverish feeling. And when Max explained that sick dragons did not get to go home, Molly flopped down on her bed and sobbed.

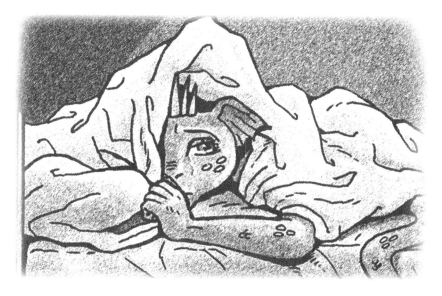

In yoga class, Nate kept farting, and every time he did, Sammie erupted with raucous laughter and fell out of her pose.

Somewhere between rec and showers, Sammie and Nate disappeared.

Max went looking. As he neared the lake, he heard clanking and shouting.

"Hah! Gotcha! Hahahaha!" Sammie yelled.

Max hurried toward the boathouse.

"Ow!" Nate rubbed his horns, reared back and took a big swing at Sammie's head with a cane sword. Sammie jumped out of the way.

Crack! The sword split in half on the corner of Mr. Yuni's workbench.

"Hey!" Max grabbed Sammie's sword. "Where did you get these?"

Nate gulped. Sammie giggled. Her mischievous green eyes betrayed her with a glance toward the broken lock on Mr. Yuni's weapons cabinet.

Max frowned. "Put those back where you found them. It's time for showers."

The pair grew quiet and followed Max's frustrated footsteps up the hill.

That night, after Max had finally corralled all five dragons into their cabins, he trudged to Mrs. Cleerheart's art studio and flopped down, frazzled and exhausted. Mrs. C served as camp nurse and art teacher. A troublemaker herself in her youth, she had a soft spot for mischievous dragons.

"Ugh!" Max let out a big sigh, and steam spewed from his nostrils. "All I want to do is sleep. Like forever." He slouched into her soft, comfy chair. The soothing fragrance of dried laven-

der calmed his nerves.

Mrs. C gave Max a kind smile and poured him a cup of Drowsy Dragon Tea that smelled of cinnamon. "Congratulations, Counselor Max! You've survived your first day."

"This morning I was full of positive energy for all of them." Max shook his head. "But now I want send two of them home and fry the other three to a crackly crunch."

Mrs. C grinned. "What did they do to you, dear?"

"Well, for starters, Nate just laughs at me. He acts like he's trying to pick a fight." Max's cheeks turned pink. "He calls me Maxine."

Mrs. C stifled a giggle. "Mr. Yuni tells me that Nate is a ferocious athlete but he has a short fuse. He goes from zero to lizard brain in two seconds."

"Why is he here?"

"Fighting at school. He accidentally broke his friend's horn off in a scuffle."

Max winced.

"His teacher believes he can learn to channel all of that energy into something positive. He's a fighter. He just needs to learn how to pick the right battles."

Max nodded. "What is Molly doing here? She seems so sweet."

"Maybe too sweet. She plays hooky to hide out from the mean girls and to mother her mother. She fell so far behind in her schoolwork that she couldn't catch up. Her principal hopes camp will help her overcome her fears and make some friends her own age."

"Hmm."

"And then there's Raif..." She watched for Max's reaction.

His nostrils flared. "I don't trust him. He's sneaky. And he completely ignores everything I say."

"They're showing you why they're here, Max." Mrs. C patted his scaly paw. "Our job is to de-code their behavior and figure out what they're trying to tell us."

Max's raised his eyebrow scales. "De-code?"

"The secret is to see through the fault to the need," she explained. "Each of these youngsters has developed their own self-protective armor. They've all been hurt in different ways, and they don't want to be hurt again."

Max took a swig of tea.

"Some are hiders, some are fighters. Some sneak around, some create distractions. Some are pleasers, some are provokers."

Max listened with interest and dread.

"But they all want to be understood. Even the ones who make

it really hard. Maybe especially them."

Max looked off into the distance. "I used to pick fights at school like Nate."

"What were you trying to communicate?"

"I was bored. And irritated by noisy dragons. And mad at my dad. Sometimes I got kicked out of class so I could sit in the hallway and read my book."

"Clever." Mrs. C grinned. "When dragons act aggressive, it usually means they feel vulnerable. Or they are in pain. They puff up to protect themselves."

Max nodded.

"And those who hide have often been hurt or humiliated."

Max's green eyes lit up with curiosity.

"Sometimes they show us what it was like at home by re-creating the same story here. The ones who were neglected by their families have an amazing way of getting lost in the shuffle here at camp. Sometimes we find ourselves neglecting them before we even realize it."

"Like Phil. I swear he's wearing a cloak of invisibility."

Mrs. C nodded.

"What's his story?"

"His teacher says he's a loner. He spends a lot of time

daydreaming and hiding in the library."

Max grinned. He liked him already.

"He comes from a big family deep in the forest. His mother died when he was a baby, and his father is rarely at home."

Max's eyes softened with sadness.

"Apparently he's an escape artist. He used to disappear for hours at school. But then he failed the same grade twice, so here he is."

"How can we help him with that?"

"He doesn't seem to have anyone who cares about him. Mr. Yuni believes we can help him feel like he matters."

Max nodded and sipped his tea.

"So, back to Raif..." Mrs. C locked eyes with Max.

He rolled his eyes back into their scales and snorted with annoyance. "He acts like he doesn't care about anything."

Mrs. C leaned forward. "Is that the whole story?"

Max sighed. "Well, there was a moment this morning when I first saw him. When he climbed out of the detention truck he looked sad and scared. Then he saw me and his eyes turned cold."

"What does he need, Max? Underneath all that snarliness and sneakiness."

"He probably needs a friend."

Mrs. C smiled.

"The thing he pretends he doesn't want is the thing he most needs."

She nodded. "I have something for you." Mrs. C opened the top drawer of her desk, pulled out a small box, and handed it to Max.

Max pried the lid off with his claws and found a set of silver dragon tags with a bright red Dragon Camp logo on the front.

"These tags have wise advise for new counselors. They may not make much sense now, but when the time comes, you'll understand."

They clinked and rattled as he flipped through and exam-

ined the mysterious symbols engraved on the back of each
tag.

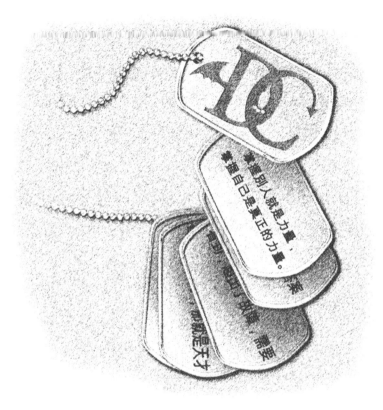

Chapter Five

On the second day of camp, Max woke up refreshed. He fastened the dragon tags around his neck and bolted out the door toward the dining hall.

A sleepy-eyed Sammie and a hyper-focused Nate sat across from one another at the dining table and gobbled up fish cakes while Raif sipped some Flaming Grass Tea and sharpened his long claws on a chunk of stone.

"Good morning, campers." Max puffed up his chest and offered his cheery greeting with a smile. "It's a beautiful day out there."

No one looked up.

Max was starving so he loaded a bowl with fragrant fish cakes, and shoveled them into his watering mouth. Mr. Yuni made the best fish cakes. Their sweet, salty, nutty crust reminded Max of holiday treats.

The dining hall door creaked open and Mrs. C appeared, followed by a timid Molly who tried to hide behind her.

Mrs. C looked around the dining hall. "Has anyone seen Phil this morning?"

The dragons looked up, looked at each other, then went back to eating.

Max jumped to his feet too fast and bumped his wooden bowl off the table. It rattled on the stone floor as a chunk of fish cake flew out of the bowl and across the room. He had completely forgotten about Phil. "Umm. I'll go check his room." He hid his flushed face and hurried to the boys' huts.

Raif smirked.

Phil was nowhere to be found. Max's heart sunk into his gut and he let out a groan.

My first duty of the day, and I've already blown it. Why am I even here? I can't do anything right.

Max's eyelid scales twitched, and suddenly he didn't like himself.

But then a familiar face came to mind. It was his old friend, Dr. Sear, who had helped him after the classroom fire.

Don't beat yourself up, Max. We all make mistakes. That's how we learn. Be gentle with yourself.

Dr. Sear had taught Max how to keep himself cool at school. She gave him a Dragonometer and warned him about Lizard Brain, the least smart and most aggressive part of a dragon's brain.

She had talked to his parents and teachers and helped them understand that Max was a special kind of dragon, sensitive and intense, with highly porous scales and super sensitive hearing. She helped Max create the insulation and privacy he needed to keep from feeling overwhelmed, and she prescribed art projects to keep him out of mischief when he was bored.

Dr. Sear had stuck by Max for many years and made sure he succeeded in school. She wasn't about to let him go to detention just because he was hotheaded.

Max took a deep breath and calmed the chatter in his head. This is all new to me. I'll get it eventually.

He released a big exhale and shook the tension out of his scales.

Now to find Phil.

Max checked every building on the campground. No Phil.

Then he walked back to the dining hall to see if Phil had magically reappeared as he often seemed to do.

Nope. No Phil. Only silence filled the empty, high-ceilinged hall.

Max slunk to the rumpus room where Mr. Yuni patiently waited to begin Aikido class.

"No sign of Phil." Max hung his head.

"We will stay on schedule." Mr. Yuni looked at his watch. "Please search the forest. The two of you can join us when you return." He blew his whistle and the other four dragons lined up at the door.

Max's chest tightened when he saw how easily the dragons followed Mr. Yuni's commands. He winced as he remembered yesterday's power struggles with Raif and Nate's ridicule.

Why don't they respect me?

Chapter Six

"Phil!" Max tromped through piles of dried leaves and sticks as he slashed a path through the dense forest with his homemade machete. The fresh fragrance of dragonberry blossoms swamped him and the morning sun blazed through the treetops and baked his back scales.

"Ow!" A razor hedge caught his tail. He stopped to disentangle it, and licked his cuts and scratches.

Max hiked and hacked and shouted for what seemed like forever. He hated getting all sweaty and sticky first thing in the morning.

Finally he reached a clearing.

Half-erased footprints led away from a small mound of dirt. When Max kicked at it, sand and soil crumbled apart to reveal ashes and blackened twigs beneath dry leaves.

"Oh, great, just what we need: a fire-breather." Max shook his head and knelt down to sniff the ashes.

They were fresh.

On the other side of the forest, Phil reclined, happily nestled into the huge, curvy branches of an ancient Waffle Nut Tree, clutching his old, tattered notebook. He watched a fluffy

flying jungle cat swoop down and catch a fresh rodent breakfast for her mewling young in a nearby tree.

Phil wished he could glide from branch to branch with such
grace. He felt like a clutzy T. Rex most of the time with his
lanky frame.

The morning sun beamed warmth through the trees while
Phil lost himself in the overlapping melodies of birdsongs and
tried to sing along. He imagined himself leading a choir of all
the birds in the forest singing in perfect harmony. It would be
the most beautiful music any dragon had ever heard.

A loud growl disrupted the angelic choir in his head. His empty stomach demanded attention.

Reluctantly, he climbed down from his blissful hideaway to go see what was for breakfast.

He sneaked into the kitchen through the back door and grabbed a bowl of fish cakes. The other dragons were already in class, so he enjoyed a leisurely breakfast out on the patio where he could listen to the birds.

The morning sun melted the last drop of tension out of Phil's muscles and his full belly pooched out as he dozed off atop the toasty cobblestone.

"There you are!" A winded, frustrated Max marched up to Phil's spot in the sun and startled him awake. "I've been looking everywhere for you. You're supposed to be in class."

Phil lifted his groggy head from the warm stone and rubbed his horns. "Huh?"

"C'mon, time to get up." Max planted an impatient paw on his hip and gestured with the other. He stood clenched while Phil rose in slow motion. This dragon must be part snail. Sheesh! "Let's go." Max launched into a brisk gait toward the Rumpus Room while Phil ambled along behind, longing for a nap and fantasizing about his next retreat to the woods.

They arrived at the doorway of Mr. Yuni's Aikido class just

in time to watch Molly topple the bigger, taller Raif in one move.

Raif fell flat on his back with a loud thud. His long, sharp tail flailed and smacked Molly in the back of the leg as she stood over him, her eyes wide with amazement.

"Ouch!" She rubbed the stinging scales on the back of her calf.

Sammie and Nate erupted with raucous laughter.

"How did you do that?" Max asked Molly. The last time he'd seen this timid little dragon she was hiding behind Mrs. C's skirt.

"I don't know." Molly stared at Mr. Yuni, bewildered.

Raif propped himself up on one elbow and smoothed out his scales. He looked up with a sly grin and winked at Molly. She blushed.

While Raif hauled his muscular frame to his feet, Mr. Yuni answered Max's question. "Aikido is not about exerting force, but rather using the force of your opponent."

Max fumed inside, frustrated that he had missed his first class because Phil had gone AWOL. He tried to shake it off and focus on Mr. Yuni.

"Molly used Raif's height and weight to defeat him," Mr. Yuni explained. "She needed only to move him off center, and then he fell like a scorchbark tree."

"Wow." Max's mouth hung open.

Mr. Yuni continued, "With Aikido, we learn to be like water, to go with the flow, to get out of the way. We allow the opponent to defeat himself."

The dragons listened with rapt attention.

Mr. Yuni jumped into fighting stance and challenged Max. "Attack!"

"What?" Max was confused.

"Charge me and try to knock me down."

Max grinned. Mr. Yuni was no match for his dragon strength. Max charged him, fueled by pent up frustration at the dragons who had disrespected him.

One millisecond before Max crashed into him, Mr. Yuni lightly touched his shoulder, pivoted backward on the ball of his left foot, and turned sideways. Max flew past him and fell on his face with a loud groan.

The dragons erupted with laughter.

Max turned red. He felt fire in his nostrils. His temperature rose. His breathing sped up.

No! Not again...

The heckling cacophony of dragon ridicule drowned out everything else as Max traveled backward through time into a daydream, all the way back to that terrible day in the classroom.

"FIRE!" Max's teacher shouted. Thick, hot smoke filled the room, and a multicolored herd of baby dragons stampeded toward the door, shaking the floor, coughing and choking.

Max froze, shocked to feel flames flying from his six-year-old nostrils.

How did I get so mad?

Most dragons couldn't breathe fire till they were much older, but Max's rage flared up fast when peers made fun of him. They liked to watch him go off. And Max had already endured so much humiliation from his bullying father that he couldn't take any more.

Ashamed of his hot temper, he scurried out the back door and disappeared into the woods while the blaze devoured his classroom.

"Are you alright, son?" Mr. Yuni's voice woke Max from his daydream. He sat on the floor, dazed. The other dragons stopped laughing and stared at him.

"Yes, sir." Max hopped up and straightened his dragon tags

"Okay, that's enough for today. Line up!" Mr. Yuni blew his whistle and the four dragons bowed to him, hurried to the door, and followed him to Mrs. C's Dragon Skills Class.

Raif looked over his shoulder at Max and snickered as he sauntered along behind the group.

Max stood alone in the middle of the room. His stomach felt queasy with shame.

What have I gotten myself into?

Chapter Seven

Five dragons fidgeted in their chairs while Mrs. C handed out their workbooks.

Sammie flipped the book open to the middle. "Aww! He's cute." She pointed at a picture of a dragon in a bubble.

"Later today we'll learn how to create an invisible bubble where we can relax and de-stress," Mrs. C explained.

"I wish I could put you in a bubble!" Nate shoved Sammie. Her chair tipped over and her workbook slid across the cobblestone floor.

Sammie pounced onto Nate's shoulders. She wrapped her stocky legs around his neck in a stranglehold. "Take it back!" She shouted and yanked on his ears.

"Ow! Get off me!" Nate swatted at Sammie's head, then lurched forward and tried to dump her off.

She laughed, clasped one of his horns between her paws and held on with all of her stubbornness.

"Okay, youngsters, let's get back to our seats!" Mrs. Cleerheart shouted, rapping her bamboo stick against a chair.

Sammie climbed off of Nate, gave him a shove, and returned to her chair. She stuck out her long, forked tongue at him and scrunched up her face.

He gave her the stink eye.

"Okay, class. Who can tell me why we're here today?"

"To learn dragon skills!" Sammie shouted with a triumphant grin.

"You have something on your nose." Nate pointed at Sammie's face. She swiped at her nose and looked at her paw.

"A little more to the left." Nate pointed. "Something brown."

"Shut up!" Sammie punched Nate's wing.

"Ouch!"

"Let's all open our workbooks to page one." Mrs. C raised her voice above the racket. "Nate, would you please read the first paragraph?"

Nate opened his book and read aloud, "Respectful Dragon Communication. At Dragon Camp we will learn to be Assertive rather than Aggressive."

Sammie snickered. Nate looked around the room. Raif rolled his eyes back into their scales.

"At Dragon Camp, we will use 'I Statements' to express our feelings.

"Thank you, Nate. Now would someone please read the examples of appropriate 'I Statements'?"

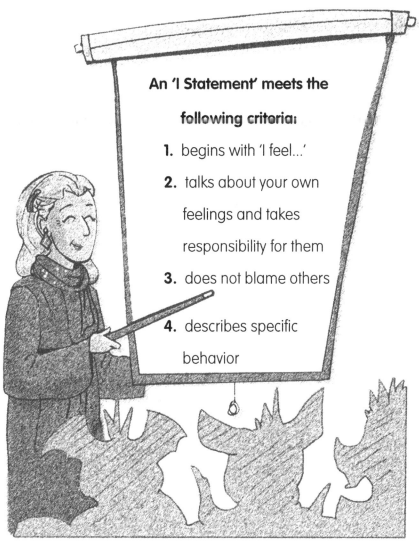

An 'I Statement' meets the following criteria:

1. begins with 'I feel...'
2. talks about your own feelings and takes responsibility for them
3. does not blame others
4. describes specific behavior

"I will." Molly volunteered in her tiny voice. "I feel hurt when you exclude me from the game and I would like to be included. I feel angry when you laugh at me and I would like you to stop."

"Thank you, Molly. Now, who would like to make their own I Statement?"

Sammie's paw shot up. "I feel Nate is a retarded reptile and I want to squish him!"

The other dragons laughed.

While Mrs. C patiently herded her unruly brood through Lesson 1, Max went looking for Mr. Yuni.

The midday sun warmed Mr. Yuni's shoulders as he sat in silence on his meditation mat. A dragonfly buzzed around his head and landed in the middle of his bald spot. Its vibrant, metallic colors glistened in the sun. Emerald green, deep turquoise, gold...

Sticks cracked and leaves crunched as Max's big scaly paws tromped toward Mr. Yuni's hut.

Mr. Yuni remained still, eyes closed.

Max stopped a few yards away and surveyed the scene. The thatched, pointed roof of the meditation hut shone like gold in the sunlight and reminded Max of the cave his mom had built for him to retreat to when he felt crispy.

Now, after a day and a half of Dragon Camp, Max longed for his cave.

The rhythm of Mr. Yuni's slow breathing and the complete calm on his face helped Max unclench. His shoulders dropped, and he felt a sense of relief. He looked up at a deep blue sky painted with perfect puffy clouds and wondered how to capture them on canvas.

Mr. Yuni brought his palms together in prayer position against his chest. Then he pressed his palms together and shot them like an arrow toward the sky. He opened his eyes and rose straight up from his cross-legged position on the sides of his feet without using his hands. The dragonfly launched up into the sky.

"Excuse me, sir." Max bowed. "I don't want to intrude, but I would like to talk with you."

"Of course, Max. Let's walk." Mr. Yuni motioned toward the waterfall trail. "What's on your mind?"

"Well..." Max felt himself flush, still embarrassed by the dragons' laughter in class, and also by his failure to keep track of Phil. He stammered. "I h-had a s-strange experience this morning." He looked over at Mr. Yuni with wide, twitchy eyes and wondered how much to tell him.

Mr. Yuni stopped walking and laid his palm on Max's chest. "Breathe, son."

Intense heat from Mr. Yuni's hand radiated through Max's torso. A sense of calm came over him. "Whoa! What was that?"

"Energy." Mr. Yuni smiled. "Please continue."

Max was puzzled, but he took a deep breath and continued his story. "When I fell down in class and the other dragons laughed at me, I felt fire in my nostrils. I was afraid I couldn't control the flames."

Mr. Yuni nodded.

"Then, all of a sudden, I traveled through time, back to when I was little."

Mr. Yuni furrowed his brow. "I wondered where you had gone. You left us for a moment."

"What happened to me?"

"It was a flashback, Max. Probably triggered by the stress of the day, the dragons' ridicule."

Max scrunched up his forehead. "Is that normal?"

"Well, it happens sometimes when old wounds are stirred up. Would you like to learn how to snap yourself out of it?"

"Yes!"

The moist shade of enormous scorchbark trees cooled off Max's scales as he hiked the rough trail beside Mr. Yuni. He could hear the roar of the falls in the distance, and wished for a splash of the cold water on his singed snout.

"Max, can you control your anger?"

The question hit Max like a stiff dragon wing upside the head. It was his worst fear.

Did Mr. Yuni doubt his fitness as a counselor? Had he totally screwed up before he even got through day two?

Max's heart sunk. The scales on his face drooped and his powerful tail flopped in the dirt.

He hung his head. "I don't know," he mumbled. Max shuffled loose dirt with the bottoms of his feet. Should I tell him about the school fire?

"Well, you can." Mr. Yuni nodded.

Max's horns spiked up.

"Max, why do we sit in meditation and focus on our breathing?"

"Um...to relax?"

"Yes, that is one reason. Deep Relaxation is very healing and energizing. But there is more."

"Like what?"

"If you can learn to control your breath, then you can also learn to calm yourself. And when you remain calm, you can control your temper."

Max's tail flicked.

"When I was a young man, I worked at the dragon school, and I saw many youngsters sent off to detention camps. They were some of the most gifted students, and they had no business living in those awful cells."

Max listened, riveted.

"Some of them returned to school, but they were never the same. Oh, they sat still and followed the rules, but their bright, fiery spirits had been dampened by too much punishment. And some of them swelled up like overripe dragon fruit from too many drugs."

Max nodded. He'd seen the bloated ones at school.

"I believe there is a better way. That is why we created Dragon Camp. Let me show you something. May I see your tags?"

Max lifted the chain up over his horns and plopped the clinking, tinkling pile of tags into Mr. Yuni's open palm.

"See this?" Mr. Yuni held up a shiny tag with a message engraved in small Chinese characters on the back.

"What does it mean?" Max leaned in.

"It is a proverb from the great Chinese philosopher, Lao Tzu."

"Mastering others is strength.
Mastering yourself is true power."

Max stared at the symbols and rubbed his hot snout.

"Cool. But what does breathing have to do with it?"

44

"Your breathing is the control panel on your dragon systems. With your breath, you can exercise mind over matter. Do you remember the Dragonometer?"

"Oh, yeah. Green is the cool zone. That's when I'm calm and relaxed, and I'm using the smartest, most creative part of my brain."

"Right. Sometimes young dragons get into trouble because they are bored or over-excited. And after they get into trouble a few times, they start to feel like bad dragons. But they are not bad. They are just misunderstood."

Max nodded.

"When a dragon gets into the red zone, he is no longer in control, his primitive lizard brain takes over. That is the least smart and most aggressive part of a dragon's brain."

Max gulped.

"The trick is to use slow, deep breathing to stay in the green zone. It all starts with the breath. Here, let's practice."

The pair sat down on a log and practiced their breathing for awhile. Max's snout cooled off, and his eyelids stopped twitching.

"Wow! That really works."

Chapter Eight

Mrs. C corralled five rambunctious dragons into her studio for arts and crafts, and Molly zoomed over to the painting she'd been working on — a portrait of a red and orange flaming lily.

Sammie and Nate found a small mountain of wet clay.

"Cool!" Sammie beamed as she shoved her paws deep into the gigantic gooey blob. Nate turned up his snout at the slimy texture and went looking for something to do.

Raif fiddled with hunks of leather and selected sharp tools for cutting and piercing it while Phil grabbed a piece of parchment and sketched the curves of the waffle nut tree where he wished he could be.

"Has everyone found something to work on?" Mrs. C asked, after a few minutes. She looked around.

Nate gave her a blank look.

"Do you have a question, Nate?"

"Um. I'm not very creative."

"Let's look outside." Mrs. C gave him a reassuring smile, and they went outside to mosey around the grounds.

"Creativity is nothing more than play, Nate. Whether you paint or write or make sculpture or work in the garden, it's all

47

an expression of your creativity. We just need to find out how your soul wants to play."

Nate's curious gaze roamed around. Patterns of shiny blue tile and polished white stones divided the gardens from the grassy areas. Chimes gonged and tinkled from scorchbark branches to discourage pests from nibbling on the vegetables.

Nate fidgeted with a string on his shirt. All he wanted was to ride his skateboard. "I wish I had a ramp."

"Great idea, Nate!" Mrs. C grinned at him.

Nate jumped, startled. He had never gotten a response like that before.

"What a perfect project for you."

"Huh?"

"Would you like to build a skateboard ramp?"

"Really?"

"Come with me." Mrs. C led Nate to the woodworking hut. It smelled of sawdust and smoke from the old wood stove. "I can show you how to use these tools, but to design the ramp we'll need some help from Mr. Yuni. He's the architect."

Mrs. C pulled some boards down from shelves and dug through a drawer full of nails while Nate explored the workshop. He could not believe she would trust him with grownup tools. At home, his dad always yelled at him to stay away from the tools and called him "irresponsible."

She showed Nate how to measure and saw the boards to size and nail them together. "See? It's easy. Now you try."

Nate hesitated.

She seemed so sure he could do it.

What if he could?

Chapter Nine

Max and Mr. Yuni hiked to the river and Max watched Mr. Yuni plunge into a deep, chilly pool under the waterfall. He dangled his feet over the edge and wished he could jump in, but with his heavy scales, he would sink straight to the bottom.

They lounged on a large slab of hot, sunbaked sandstone and watched the falling water glisten in the sun as it sprayed them with a refreshing cloud of mist. The rushing river drowned out the other sounds of the forest.

Mr. Yuni gazed into a clear sky framed by treetops, and breathed in the spicy fragrance of evergreens.

"You know, Max, throughout history most of the great artists and geniuses were like our young dragons at one time. They didn't fit in, and most of them were misunderstood." He stretched his hairy arms behind his head and made a pillow with his clasped hands.

Max propped himself up on his scaly elbows.

Mr. Yuni continued. "Your job this summer is to survive. It won't always be easy, but you will succeed, and you will change the lives of some of these young geniuses."

Max raised his eyebrow scales. "Survive?"

"Yes. They will test you with outrageous behavior and sometimes you will want to roast them to a crackly crunch."

Max clenched up all over. He hadn't realized that he would confront his own demons.

"Surviving means this: don't abandon and don't retaliate. No matter what they do to you, stay cool and stay put. When they see that you are strong and kind, they will settle down and get to work."

Max caught himself holding his breath and released it with a big whoosh.

"But they will test the horns off of you first." Mr. Yuni winked.

They lounged in the sun for awhile and listened to the falls. The sound of water gushing over the rocks soothed Max's senses.

While Max relaxed with Mr. Yuni, Raif sneaked off into the woods. It was only the second day of camp and he was already bored out of his mind.

What am I going to do in this place all summer?

He blew an exasperated blast of fire out of his nostrils at a nearby dragonberry bush.

The bush exploded. Its dry branches cracked and popped in the heat. Raif stared at the flames, mesmerized. He loved fire.

As the bush shrunk down to smoldering embers, he awoke from his trance and fired up another one. This time, a bigger one.

Raif leaned against an old arrowroot tree while the fire crackled and hissed. His tail flicked with excitement as the flames licked the branches and leaves. They reached out with long, orange, forked tongues like they wanted to devour the

whole forest.

He gnawed on a piece of bark and savored the blaze.

While the other dragons went off to enjoy their free time, Molly stayed with her painting. She lost herself in the reds and oranges of the flaming lilies, and layered color upon texture to capture every shadow she imagined between their petals in the late afternoon low light .

Time disappeared and, after a while, Mrs. Cleerheart came tip-toeing back into the studio to check on her. She sneaked a peek at the painting over Molly's shoulder. "Wow."

Molly jumped.

"Oh, I'm sorry, dear. I didn't mean to startle you. It's just so beautiful!"

Molly blushed.

"You have a gift."

"Thank you." Molly squeaked in her tiny voice.

"Aren't you getting hungry, dear? It's half past noon, and we're almost finished with lunch."

"Oh." Molly suddenly noticed her stomach growling.

Mrs. C grinned. "You were in the zone."

Molly looked scared. "Is that okay?"

"Oh, it's more than okay. It's the best place an artist can go. And you, Miss Molly, are a true artist."

Molly stared.

"We're going to have a lot of fun this summer." Mrs. C motioned all around the studio. "But first, let's get you some nourishment."

Mrs. C patted Molly's shoulder and walked beside her to the dining hall.

Molly felt like she was in a dream.

An artist? Me?

It sounded so important, and she'd never been important before.

Chapter Ten

When Molly and Mrs. C arrived at the dining hall, they found it empty except for some dirty dishes on the table.

"Looks like someone forgot to clean up." Mrs. C propped her fists on her hips and frowned.

Molly found a clean bowl and some fish cakes, and sat down at the end of the dirty table. She turned up her snout at the mess.

"Enjoy your lunch, dear. I'm going dragon hunting."

As Mrs. C stalked down the path toward the lake, she heard a loud thud followed by a shout. She picked up her pace.

Atop the splintery old boat dock, Raif stood over Nate with a smirk on his handsome face as he tightened the strings on a pair of boxing gloves.

"Get up, Nate!" Sammie shouted.

Phil sat at the end of the dock, dangled his paws in the water, and ignored the noise. He tossed a stone into the lake, and watched the water ripple out in circles.

Nate jumped up from the spot where Raif had knocked him down. He rubbed a sore spot on his tail, pulled the boxing gloves tighter on his paws, and took a wild swing at his opponent's head. Raif dodged the punch.

Nate swung again, first with his right paw, then his left, his face scales red with fury. He was too mad to take proper aim.

Raif stepped back with a grin and watched Nate reel from the momentum of his own spazzy swinging.

Nate fell to his knees with a thunk and smacked his glove on the dock with a frustrated roar.

Sammie giggled.

Mrs. C clomped onto the dock in her work boots.

Raif jerked around.

Mrs. C looked down at Nate. "Are you okay?"

"Yeah." He shook out his sweaty scales.

She held out her hand. He ignored it and jumped to his feet.

"It's quiet time now," she announced in a stern voice. "Nate, Sammie, go to your cabins. Raif, come with me."

As Sammie and Nate scampered off to their rooms, they looked back at Raif stomping along behind Mrs. C toward the dining hall, his neck stiff and his chest puffed out like a pigeon.

"He's in trouble!" Sammie grinned.

Nate grunted and headed toward his cabin.

Phil sneaked off into the woods.

"Please clear the dishes and wash them, Raif. For the rest of the week you'll be in charge of clean up."

Raif scowled and gathered the dirty bowls.

"As the oldest in the group, you're the one these young dragons look up to, Raif. They follow your example."

He rolled his eyes.

"So, where did you learn to box like that?"

Raif's head popped up. He studied her expression. What does she want?

Raif didn't trust her. She was probably fake, like all the others.

"Detention," he mumbled.

"Well, you're very good. Have you ever considered boxing competitively?"

His tail flicked.

"Have you heard about the tournament? Mr. Yuni goes every year."

"Nuh-uh."

"How long have you lived at the detention camp, Raif?"

"Dunno."

Mrs. C shook her head. "You must have missed out on a lot, being so isolated from the world."

Raif shrugged, and hauled a basketful of dirty bowls to the

wash bucket.

"Mr. Yuni trains young boxers. He was a champion himself when he was a young man."

Raif's horns spiked up.

"Would you like me to talk to him about training you?"

Raif washed a dish. He wasn't about to let anyone trick him into getting his hopes up.

"Of course, you would have to follow the rules and take care of your responsibilities while you train."

Raif felt a familiar old tug of war in his chest. He didn't like do-gooders. They always had an agenda. Too many strings attached.

And he had lied about the tournament. Of course he knew about it. It was the only thing he had ever really wanted to do.

Max returned to camp very relaxed. Lucky for him, it was still quiet time, so he lay down in the shade before afternoon rec.

He had just dozed off when the bell rang to summon all dragons to the rec field.

Mr. Yuni blew his whistle. "Line up!"

All five dragons scurried to get in line.

59

Max shook his head. *I wonder if they'll ever listen to me like that.*

"Today we're going to work on building trust," Mr. Yuni announced.

"Ugh." Raif sighed under his breath. *What a load of dragon scat.*

"Pair off, please. Max, I want you with Molly. Raif, you go with Nate. Phil, you go with Sammie."

"No way!" Nate shouted. "He just tried to bust my head open."

"All the more reason to work on building trust," Mr. Yuni replied. "Please make two lines of three and face your partner."

Molly stood across from Max and blushed.

Nate puffed up his chest and polished his horns while Raif sharpened one of his claws.

Phil watched a spikey, red hornet bird flit from flower to flower around the edge of the rec field. Its tiny wings buzzed as it flew.

"Our first exercise is a simple fall. Let me demonstrate. Phil, please turn around with your back toward me. At the count of three, fall backward into my arms and I will catch you."

Phil shuffled around and followed Mr. Yuni's instructions. He looked up at the wispy clouds that floated across the sky while Mr. Yuni counted. The sun warmed his scales and relaxed his shoulders as he fell back into Mr. Yuni's secure embrace.

Ahh...is it nap time yet?

One by one the dragons fell and caught each other. Until it was Raif's turn to be caught.

Raif looked at Nate, crossed his scaly arms against his chest, and shook his head.

"Is there a problem, Raif?" Mr. Yuni asked.

"I don't trust him."

"Well, I didn't trust you either, and I had to do it!" Nate propped his paws on his hips.

"Raif, come over here, please."

Raif walked toward Mr. Yuni and stood claw to toe with him.

Mr. Yuni placed his left hand on Raif's shoulder and his right palm on Raif's heart. "The longest journey begins with one step, son." Mr. Yuni spoke softly and looked deep into Raif's guarded, pale blue eyes.

Raif peered into Mr. Yuni's dark eyes. Heat radiated from Mr. Yuni's hands and sent an electric current through Raif's chest. His eyes grew wide and his horns spiked up.

"So, Raif, when you feel ready, please turn and fall into my arms. I will catch you."

Raif felt a strange sense of calm, held by an unfamiliar force. He turned around and, for the first time, he let go.

After a few more trust-building exercises, Mr. Yuni released the dragons for free time. Nate and Sammie went wading in the lake and took turns trying to drown each other in the shallow water.

Phil wandered off into the forest while Molly made a bee-line for the art studio.

Raif felt weird. Normally, his favorite thing was making fires in the woods during free time. But today he didn't feel like it. For the first time, he didn't feel like being alone.

He sat on the beach and watched Sammie and Nate play. Melancholy filled his throat. Raif had never really played before. Between foster homes and detention, there weren't many chances.

Boxing matches in detention were about as close as he got to play.

Mr. Yuni and Mrs. Cleerheart retreated to the garden for some dragonberry tea while the youngsters enjoyed their free time.

"How is Raif doing?" Mr. Yuni asked.

"Well, I caught him boxing with Nate this afternoon when he was supposed to be cleaning up. He was pretty rough on him."

"He comes from a tough background." He looked down into his tea. "On our way back from the falls this morning, I saw some charred bushes."

"Uh-oh." Mrs. C's forehead crinkled. "I hope we can keep him here. I fear this might be his last chance."

Mr. Yuni nodded. "Poor dragon never had a chance. He believes there is nothing to look forward to."

Mrs. C perked up. "You know what? Raif has a talent for boxing. I wonder if he has any passion for it."

"Have you seen him move?"

Mrs. C grinned. "He's good."

"But can we keep him from burning down the camp long enough to train him for the tournament?"

She scrunched up her face. "Let's give him a chance." Mrs. C leaned forward in her chair. "We can keep a close eye on him."

Mr. Yuni looked out at the dry forest. Is it really worth risking all of them to try to save one?

Chapter Eleven

That evening at dinner, the dragons were quiet, which made Mrs. C wonder what they were up to.

Sammie hunched over her bowl and gobbled up a huge chunk of fresh fish pie as though she hadn't eaten for days. She'd been getting chunky around the middle since she started taking behavior drugs. They toned down her wild outbursts, but made her feel hungry all the time.

Sammie licked her bowl clean with a loud slurp, let out a big burp, and sniffed around for more pie. Her mouth watering, she reached for the last remaining slice. Nate grabbed it and stuffed it into his mouth. She glowered at him. He shot her a victorious grin, his full cheeks puffed out like a chipmunk.

Sammie shoved her chair aside and stalked out the door. She was bored.

Sammie was the kind of dragon who liked a lot of excitement, and when she couldn't find any, she would stir some up.

Fighting with Nate was getting old, so she went looking for adventure in the woods.

The late afternoon sun turned the leaves orange and yellow like fire, and long shadows crept around glowing tree trunks.

"This place is so boring." Sammie muttered as she tromped through dry leaves.

She wished she could find some spiky reptiles to play with, or at least a cool cave to explore.

Sammie hated being a girl dragon. The boys got to have all the fun. And now that they were getting older, the boys didn't want her to play with them anymore. They liked the girlie-girl dragons. The ones who didn't fight with them. How boring could you get?

Sammie stomped along, grumbling to herself about how unfair it all was. She wished she could go home. At least there she could ride her skateboard all day, even if she didn't have any friends. She remembered the day when she ran around the school naked, climbed up on the roof, and threatened to jump off. The teachers were afraid of her after that, and sent her to Dragon Camp.

"Ow!" One of her horns caught on a tree branch. She grabbed the branch, broke it off, and marched on.

After dinner, Phil dug a tattered, musty notebook out of his bag and slipped away to his favorite hideout in the engulfing arms of the old scorchbark tree.

He loved this time of day when the setting sun transformed the colors of the forest with its rose-colored glow.

Phil climbed up into his private tree cradle and scooted around to get comfortable. With his full belly and massive tail, it took some wiggling to find just the right spot. A soft breeze rustled the leaves and carried the scent of summer blossoms to his nostrils.

"Ahh." Phil reclined against the tree trunk and tuned in to the choir of birdsong that enveloped the forest in a soothing blanket of sound. I wonder why the evening choir sounds so different from the morning choir. Maybe they're tired.

Phil opened his old notebook and searched for a clean page. Most of the book was already full of drawings and barely legible, tiny words scrawled in charcoal.

He pulled a nub of charcoal out of its hiding place inside the book binding and sharpened it on the scorch bark.

At the top of the page Phil printed, The Secret Lives of Dragons. He had an idea for a story about the other campers. Some of them seemed easy to understand, but others seemed more complicated.

Like Max. He seemed so together, so confident, but when no one else was looking, his anxious eyes darted around.

Maybe Max's secret is that he's afraid all the time.

Phil remembered how spooked Max looked when he fell down in the Aikido class. Yep. Fear. That's Max's secret.

Phil listed his characters and pretended to telepathically sniff out their hidden truths.

But when it came to Molly, he got butterflies in his stomach. She was such a sweet, pretty girl. And such a talented artist. If only he had the courage to talk to her.

Maybe he could write to her. Or better still, maybe he could make a picture for her. An artist could make something for another artist, right?

Phil sighed. Why did girls have to be so confusing?

Chapter 12

As the last drop of orange-pink sunset disappeared behind the treetops, Mr. Yuni banged the gong to summon the dragons for evening meditation. One by one they appeared and took their places on the faded straw mats that Mrs. C had woven years before.

When it was time to begin, Sammie's mat was still empty.

Mrs. C strode outside and shouted, "Sammie!" She banged the gong again.

Mr. Yuni stuck his head out the door. "Come on in. Let's get started. She'll turn up."

Mrs. C frowned and looked out at the dark forest.

Mr. Yuni reassured her, "If she doesn't appear soon, we'll go looking. Come inside."

While the dragons inhaled and exhaled together, Mrs. C worried. She had a bad feeling in the pit of her stomach. Something wasn't right.

Mr. Yuni dimmed the lights, lit a spicy candle, and led the group through a guided meditation. He asked them to visualize their ideal life in five years. A warm breeze blew in through the open door. The candle flame danced and smoked.

Max imagined an exhibit of his paintings. He could hear

the ooh's and ahh's of the crowd as they admired his work.

Nate saw himself at a skateboard competition collecting a gigantic gold trophy almost as big as he was.

Molly tried to imagine something to look forward to.

Raif rolled his eyes and looked around the room.

But Phil's imagination got stuck. He could only see Sammie.

Startled by the image that appeared in his mind's eye, his eyelid scales popped open and he looked over at Mrs. Cleerheart. She looked back at him.

While the other dragons sat in silence with Mr. Yuni, Phil motioned for Mrs. C to follow him.

She nodded, and the two rose without a sound and tiptoed outside.

Raif crept out behind them, hid behind the doorframe, and eavesdropped.

Phil's breathing sped up and his eyes grew wide.

"What is it, Phil?"

"I saw Sammie. She's upside down by the water."

"I saw the same thing."

Before either of them could utter another word, a flurry of color flew past them. Raif bounded out the doorway and sprinted into the forest.

Sparks flew from Raif's nostrils and left a trail of light like an army of fireflies behind him as he disappeared into the dark wood.

"Help!" Sammie struggled to catch her breath, her voice hoarse from shouting. "Help!" Her ankle throbbed where the tree roots held her, stuck and twisted on the riverbank. She longed to wiggle loose from their clutches, but then she would fall, head first, onto sharp rocks far below.

She tried to raise her voice again to shout for help, but it was no use. The rushing and pounding of the waterfall drowned out any sound she could make.

She burst into spasms of sobbing and gasped for air as hot tears flowed down her forehead scales and dripped off of her upside-down horns.

One of the roots that held her leg cracked and dropped her a few inches lower with a jolt. Sammie screamed. Searing pain shot up her leg and she moaned. Terror clenched her throat.

She closed her eyes. Please help me.

She pictured her family back home. They'd never understood her. And her school, where they said she was crazy, and her new friend Nate, who didn't try to change her.

And she saw those stupid dragonberries that hung out over the edge of the riverbank and had lured her into this mess. How was she supposed to know the cliff would crumble like a fish cake?

Sammie hung in the dark against the cold clay of the river-bank. Falls raged above and a cold river rushed below. Her parched throat hurt. Roots poked her in the back.

The only thing more terrifying than being stuck in this trap was sliding out of it.

Raif dodged trees, leapt rocks. He swatted bushes and branches out of his way as he bounded toward the falls as fast as his powerful legs would take him. He'd had a feeling that crazy little dragon would get herself into trouble.

Raif got a kick out of Sammie's and Nate's antics. They showed him what it was like to be young and carefree. They had no fear, and they didn't worry about anything besides having fun. Sort of the opposite of Raif's life. Even though they were only a few years apart in age, to Raif, it felt like a lifetime.

As Raif neared the river, he felt around on the ground for dry branches. He stuffed as many leaves as he could between a handful of sticks and snorted out a quick blast of fire to set the torch aflame.

He clutched the light in his paw and approached the river's edge with caution.

"Sammie!" he shouted and held the torch out over the edge. He knelt and stretched his long arms out to sweep the bank with torchlight, squinting at the rocks below. No sign of Sammie.

The piercing screech of a nearby owl startled Raif. He dropped the torch. It caught on roots that stuck out from the river bank, and hung for a moment like a lantern, reflected in the dark water below.

A gust of wind swept a sheet of cold spray up from the falls. It doused Raif and snuffed out the torch. He shook off the water.

Raif heard another screech from a few yards downstream and followed the sound. Strange for an owl to perch so close to the river.

"SCREEEEEECH!" The moonlight illuminated a tiny owl who stared, bug-eyed at Raif. He tiptoed carefully along the crumbly cliff toward the noisy messenger.

When he was just a few feet away, the owl launched off the branch and disappeared into the forest.

Raif heard sobbing. He knelt and strained to see.

He sprinted back to the forest, assembled another torch, and breathed a big blast of fire to set it aflame.

But before he could return to search for Sammie, a face appeared in the glow of his torchlight.

Chapter 13

Mr. Yuni stared at Raif with fire in his eyes. He snatched the torch out of Raif's claws.

Raif grabbed back the torch and ran to the river.

"Hey!" Mr. Yuni called. Frowning, he stepped carefully over rocks and fallen branches, mindful of his weak ankles. Max followed close behind.

Raif reached the riverbank, breathless, and stretched his long, muscular torso over the edge. He held the light down as far as he could reach toward the spot where he had heard the crying. He moved the torch slowly along the bank. "Sammie?"

"Help!" A faint cry came from below. Raif scooted along wet clay, further toward the edge, the torch dangling from his claws. He could barely make out the shadow of Sammie's long tail as she hung upside down against the riverbank.

"Sammie!"

"I'm here."

"Sammie, it's Raif."

"My leg is stuck."

"Hold on. I'm coming to get you." Raif shoved the end of his torch into the mud and climbed down to her. "Hold on to me."

He gently loosened the roots that held her injured leg.

Sammie climbed onto Raif's strong back and wrapped her arms around his neck. She clamped her good leg around his waist while the injured leg dangled to the side.

Raif liked the feeling of Sammie's trusting arms wrapped around him. It was the closest thing to a hug that he had felt in a long time.

As the light from his torch faded, Raif sank his claws into the cold clay of the riverbank and felt around for protruding roots to use as steps and handles.

He wished he could launch into flight, soar high above the trees and Mr. Yuni, and carry Sammie back to camp, but there was no way to take off safely from a muddy riverbank with a heavy load.

Raif planted his right paw on a fat root and reached out with his left leg to find another. He groped around in the dark with his claws, barely balancing his weight in midair.

Just as his left paw located another root, his right paw slid off the slippery wood. He lurched backward and grasped for another root. Sammie lost her grip around his neck. She screamed and grabbed at his wings.

"Ouch!" Raif winced as Sammie climbed up one of his wings and clutched his neck again.

"Sorry," she sputtered as she struggled.

Raif gasped. "You're choking me!"

Sammie panted, winced from the pain in her leg, and tried to breathe. "Sorry," she squeaked.

"Hold on tight. We're going up."

Raif carefully climbed to the top of the riverbank, hauling

his precious cargo. He didn't care if Mr. Yuni was mad at him for playing with fire. He was used to getting in trouble for everything. You can't win with humans. They can't be pleased, so why try,

Chapter 14

During the next few days, Mr. Yuni helped Nate design a skateboard ramp. They worked together every afternoon to shape and sand it. Nate dubbed it Death Ramp and painted it black with a pterodactyl skeleton in the middle.

When no one was looking, Sammie carved her name into the side.

Between classes, skateboarding, Aikido lessons, and watching Raif train, Sammie and Nate didn't have much time to get into mischief.

But they still managed.

Sammie was obsessed with boxing and with Raif, and she did not understand why Mr. Yuni wouldn't let her train for the boxing tournament. Aikido was boring.

One afternoon, after Mr. Yuni had retreated to his hut for a nap, Sammie and Nate sneaked into the boathouse and broke into his collection of boxing gloves. They tried to mimic the moves Raif was working on, but mostly they just got bruised up and made each other mad.

Mrs. C had been reading the poems Phil wrote in class and recognized his talent. She constructed a book of clean parchment to replace the musty, old crammed-full notebook he carried around.

Phil was grateful for the new paper, but he still carried his old book around.

Mrs. C excused Phil from some of the camp activities so that he could spend more time writing. She figured if Raif could be excused for boxing, the artists deserved equal treatment.

And besides, she could always count on Phil to reappear at the next meal.

No one knew where Phil disappeared to for hours, and they weren't interested. But Max was curious. Fascinated by Phil's cloak of invisibility, he wished he had one of his own. He could wear it during sparring practice.

One afternoon he followed Phil and watched him climb up into the secret tree.

Max smiled at the sight of Phil's long tail hanging down from his hiding place, swinging lazily in the sun.

That's perfect. A dragon in his element.

Then he had an epiphany.

That's it! That's my art school project: Dragons In Their Element.

He thought about his young charges' quirks and lit up with a big grin. They would provide some great material.

He nestled into a comfortable spot in the shade, stretched out his tail, and opened up his sketchbook. Leaves overhead swished and whispered in the breeze and birds sang softly in the afternoon sun.

While Phil lost himself in writing, Max disappeared into his drawing: a peaceful, magical hideaway, with hornet birds and flying squirrels, and a very happy dragon writing poetry in his tree.

Chapter 15

The next day Mr. Yuni fitted Max with a face guard and chest pad for sparring with Raif. It wasn't fair, but Max was the only one big enough to do the job safely. Mr. Yuni had amazing moves, but he was getting old and his ankles were weak.

During the first week of training, Mr. Yuni focused on footwork. Max already knew most of the moves from boxing lessons, but Raif had a lot to learn. He'd never had a real lesson before, but had picked up some moves from the other dragons in detention.

Max enjoyed knowing more than Raif. For once, Raif couldn't ridicule him.

Day after day, Raif struggled to learn new footwork. Mr. Yuni called out drills and shouted a thousand times, "Side to side! Side to side!"

Max quickly grew bored. These steps were too easy. Raif was such a klutz. It was like dancing with a T Rex. He must have relied on brute strength to fight in detention, because he sure couldn't move.

"Raif!" Mr. Yuni barked. "You must practice these steps every day until they come naturally. If you don't learn to stick and move, you'll get clobbered in the arena. Your style may have worked in detention, but at the tournament level, it is dangerous."

Raif turned red.

Max smirked.

"Again!" Mr. Yuni ordered.

"Excuse me, sir, but can't Raif practice footwork on his own? He doesn't really need me for this, and I have more important things to do."

Raif's nostrils flared and his face scales turned a deeper shade of red.

Mr. Yuni intervened. "Let's go through it one more time. Then we'll take a break."

Raif glared at Max with blazing eyes. Just another spoiled brat who had everything handed to him.

Max mindlessly demonstrated the same steps one more time while Raif hyper-focused to get them just right. Raif did better when he was mad.

Mr. Yuni watched them move in synchrony. He could feel their aggressive energy like the heat coming off of a furnace. The muscles in his neck tightened. These two together are a recipe either for greatness or disaster.

After boxing lessons came free time, and Max hurried to the art studio before Mr. Yuni could find more unpleasant jobs for him to do.

He arrived to find Molly alone, working on her painting, and tapped softly on the doorframe to avoid startling her. She jumped anyway. Molly was a twitchy one.

"It's looking good." Max admired her work and nodded.

She blushed. "Thank you."

Max grabbed an easel from the corner and set up to make a painting of his own. Inspired by Dragons in their Element, he imagined a wall full of colorful portraits that would impress the art school people.

Molly watched Max work until her curiosity overcame her shyness. "What are you doing?"

Max smiled. "It's for art school."

"Wow." Molly stared. "Art school?"

"Yeah. Mrs. C is helping me get in. It's part of the camp counselor deal."

Molly's eyes grew wide.

"What about you? Do you want to go to art school some-day?"

Molly gulped and shook her head so hard that her horns wiggled. "I could never do that."

"Why not?"

"I'd be too afraid of making a fool of myself."

"But you're really good, Molly."

"Really?" She stood in silence while she did cartwheels in her head.

"What do you paint besides flowers?"

Molly blushed. "Umm. I don't know."

"You've never painted before?" Max raised his forehead

scales.

Molly shook her head.

"Dang, girl, if this is your first try, you really are good."

Molly looked at her painting. She had no idea if it was any good. She just liked the vibrant colors and shadowy contours of the fire lilies.

"Why don't you try painting some other stuff? I can teach you how to make trees if you want."

"Really?"

"Here, I'll show you. It's easy."

Max's paw rattled around in a can of brushes, his claws clicking against the tin, until he found what he was looking for. He pulled out an old, worn fan brush and held it up to the light where Molly could see it.

Molly felt the stiff bristles with her thumb and brushed them across her paw.

"Here's how you make a scorchbark tree." Max dipped a few dry bristle tips in charcoal colored paint and sketched a tree trunk in the middle of the canvas.

"Wow. That's cool. It doesn't take very long."

"Nope, it's quick. This brush is a good shortcut. Now watch this." Max rinsed out the brush in a cup of water and dabbed it with a rag. Then he scrunched up the damp bristles between his fingers.

Molly leaned closer.

He dipped the scrunched up bristles into yellow then green. Moving briskly, he dabbed the brush all around the limbs of the scorchbark tree until it came alive with spring leaves.

"That's amazing!" Molly raised her eyebrow scales. "It's like magic."

"The magic is learning technique. Mrs. C taught me. Now you try." Max handed her the brush and grabbed another one for himself.

Together they filled the canvas with tree after tree using every color on the palette. Their colors grew wilder as they went along, and they laughed at the hot pink leaves and passionate purple tree trunks. Molly even made a rainbow tree with a multicolored trunk.

Soon the canvas was too full for even one more colorful leaf. They stood back and admired their masterpiece.

"Your first forest." Max waved toward the painting with a warm smile.

Molly laughed. "My psychedelic forest."

"It's awesome." Max nodded his approval. "Maybe needs a little more light up here." He dabbed a few more patches of yellow sunlight on the leaves.

Molly felt all warm and fulfilled as she looked at their creation. "Do you know how to make birds?"

"Sure." Max reached for some bird-colored paints. But before he could get started, the dinner bell clanged and jarred them out of their creative reverie.

"Omigod! Dinner time already?" Molly looked out the window. "Max! Look!"

Max hurried to the window and looked over Molly's shoulder at the pink-orange-red sunset.

"The leaves really are pink!" Molly had never felt such joy.

"Cool." Max relaxed into a contented smile as they admired a forest animated by the reflected colors of the setting sun.

Chapter 16

The dining room was quiet that evening. Everyone was tired, and Sammie had a terrible headache from Nate punching her.

After cleanup, they took a stroll outside to enjoy the cool evening air. Phil gathered sticks for a bonfire.

Raif sneaked off into the woods. It was getting to be too much togetherness for him. He was used to spending a lot of time alone in his detention cell. And it felt amazing to be out in the woods.

Ever since that night on the riverbank, Raif had been wondering about something.

Most dragons could not fly until they were fully grown. For Raif, that would be another year or two.

But he had always been ahead of schedule. He had walked early, talked early, and breathed fire ridiculously early.

Raif was curious.

And that riverbank was the perfect place to experiment. At least there was no "zero tolerance" policy on flying. He smirked.

Raif arrived at the river's edge and searched for a soft landing spot, away from the sharp rocks. The sun was almost gone, so he wouldn't have much time to practice.

He hiked downstream and spotted a sandy beach, just wide enough for a landing strip.

Raif stood atop the riverbank and extended his wings into the wind. They stretched twenty feet wide, and caught a gust that scooped him up a few feet off the ground.

"Whoa!" He quickly tucked his wings back in, dropped with a thud, and caught his breath.

He examined his right wing. "I wonder how you steer these things." Very slowly he stretched and extended, and leaned forward toward the river.

The wind whipped and swept Raif high up in the air.

"Ahh!" He looked down at the riverbank below.

He rocked back and forth, tossed by the breeze, and felt the immense power of his huge wings.

"Okay, here goes." He leaned forward. A sudden tail wind propelled him out over the river.

"Ahhh!" In a frightened reflex, he jerked his wings to his sides and plunged into the cold, deep pool. His heavy, scaled reptile frame sank.

Raif's scales stiffened and hurt as the cold water bent them back. His heart pounded, his stomach knotted, and his throat clenched tight. His lungs ached for a breath of air.

Part of him wanted to curl up in a ball and sink to the bottom of the river. Who would care anyway? He didn't have any family. And nowhere to go but detention. And nothing to look forward to really.

Why bother?

Sinking fast in the dark, Raif knew that if he did not change direction, he would die.

"Use your wings." A still, small voice whispered in Raif's heart.

Who...? He realized he was not alone.

Raif mustered all his strength and forced his wings to extend a bit to slow his downward plummet. As he slowed, he struggled to stretch them out a little further.

With a watery grunt, Raif put all of his muscle into the biggest wing flap he could muster.

He began to rise.

Up, up, up he rose, defying the immense darkness, one wing flap at a time.

His lungs hurt and his muscles burned as he fought his way toward the light.

As he ascended, images flashed in Raif's mind... Sammie's goofy grin...Mrs. C's kind eyes.

An ember lit up in his heart.

He forced his tired muscles to push against the water, and continued to rise.

Just when he couldn't hold his breath any longer, his wings burst out of the water with an explosive splash. He gasped and filled his burning lungs with fresh air.

Exhausted, Raif fully extended his wings into a giant purple raft and lay back on top of the water.

Chapter 17

"Where's Raif?" Sammie sniffed around the campground, searching for signs of her friend.

It was dark, and she wanted to sit by him at the bonfire.

Max patted her shoulder. "He'll be fine, Sammie. He's probably just out taking a walk." Out burning down the forest more likely. Max tried not to roll his eyes. "Here, come sit by the fire with Mrs. Cleerheart. I'll go look for him."

"Okay." Sammie huddled up close to the fire to get warm.

Max resented Raif. First, he had violated the fire-breathing ban so he shouldn't even be here. Then he had ridiculed Max in front of everyone – Max's worst nightmare.

Then he sucked up all of Max's free time with remedial boxing lessons. And now I have to waste a perfectly good evening tracking him down? I'd rather let him rot.

Just as Max finished preparing a lantern for his search, Raif emerged from the woods looking like a giant drowned bat.

"Raif!" Sammie sprang from her seat, threw off her blanket, and ran to him. She slammed into his wet torso and clamped her stubby arms around his middle as if she would never let go. "I was worried." Her words were muffled by Raif's armpit, where her head was lodged.

"I'm okay, little one. Just went for a swim." His voice was weak; not very convincing.

Sammie looked up and studied his face. "Dragons can't swim!"

"Yeah, I kinda figured that out." Raif winked at her and shuffled over to the fire, shaking from the cold.

Sammie ran after him, grabbed her discarded blanket off the ground, and draped it around Raif's broad shoulders.

"Thanks, kid." He gave her a weary smile.

The other dragons watched while Sammie molded herself into his side as though they were fused, hip to wing. The pair stared into the flames.

Chapter 18

The next day, Mr. Yuni decided to give footwork a rest before Max and Raif roasted each other. He took Raif aside to work on speed drills while Max painted.

Mr. Yuni had always loved boxing, and training young talent took him back to his own victories. Raif's fearless defiance reminded him of his younger self. That trait had made him a great fighter.

Like Raif, Mr. Yuni had grown up without a family, and he had learned early to act tough and trust no one. But as a young man, he had found a friend.

Coach Shonen had a gift for spotting potential in young rebels like Hiroaki Yuni. He'd been redeeming them for decades. And though Hiroaki resisted at first, Coach Shonen persisted.

With patience and time, he broke through young Hiroaki's protective armor and connected with his strong heart.

Shonen and Yuni won many contests together. And when the wise old coach passed on to the next life, he left a case full of boxing gloves to his beloved apprentice.

Mr. Yuni didn't tell Raif, but the gloves he'd given him were the ones he'd worn in his first tournament – a tournament he had won, even though he was younger and smaller than the other boys.

He won because he was fearless and he was fast.

Raif already had the fearless part down. Now they needed to work on fast.

Mr. Yuni's drills seemed impossible at first. Raif punched the bag as speedily as he could until he was breathless. Mr. Yuni shouted, "Faster!"

Raif jumped rope so rapidly his legs burned and his tail muscles ached. Mr. Yuni yelled, "Jump faster!"

Day after day, Yuni pushed. He pushed and pushed until he stretched Raif beyond all his beliefs about what he was capable of.

Finally the day came when he stopped shouting. At the end of Raif's workout, he grinned. "Now you are fast."

A smile emerged in Raif's heart. He tried to hide it, but it was too big to contain and spread all over his face.

Chapter 19

In the days leading up to the tournament, Max returned to sparring practice with Raif who needed to perfect his footwork. Max hated to waste precious summer days on boxing, but he wanted to be a good counselor.

The pair punched and blocked and ducked and wove while Mr. Yuni watched and shouted corrections.

Raif had improved a lot, and he enjoyed showing Max up.

One afternoon during practice, Max's face guard rattled loose and distracted him for a moment - just enough time for Raif to sock him on the chin and send the mask flying into the lake with a splash.

Max fumed.

Raif smirked.

When Max saw the gleam of ridicule in Raif's eyes, his temperature rose.

"Getting a little overheated, Maxine?" Raif taunted him. "Maybe you should take a time out."

Max's mind went red. He ripped off his gloves, swiped at Raif with his powerful claws, and slashed his face scales.

Mr. Yuni rushed toward them. "Stop!"

Raif's eyes bugged out with panic. He tried to get away.

But before he could turn and run, a blast of fire exploded from
Max's nostrils and roasted Raif's face and neck.

Raif yowled in pain. His hide hissed. Smoke rose from his
singed, smelly scales.

Max gawked at Raif's blackened, bloody face in horror.

Mr. Yuni jumped onto the dock, pulled Raif into the shallow
lake, and cradled his head in the crook of his arm while he
bathed the singed scales with cold water. With angry flames
in his dark eyes he barked at Max. "Find Mrs. Cleerheart.
Tell her to prepare burn ointment."

"Yes, sir." Max bolted toward Mrs. C's studio, his heart pounding in his throat.

It was just like that day in the classroom so many years ago. He hadn't meant to get so hot. He didn't even realize what was happening until it was too late.

Oh my god. What have I done?

Max's chest tightened and his stomach felt queasy. He arrived at Mrs. C's doorway sweaty and out of breath.

The other dragons heard Max panting and looked up from their art projects.

Mrs. C dropped her paintbrush and ran outside.

"It's Raif." Max choked on shame as he forced the words out. "I burned him. Mr. Yuni needs burn ointment. For his face."

Mrs. C placed a reassuring hand on Max's shoulder. "Come with me."

Four curious dragon faces popped out the window to watch.

Mrs. C shooed them away. "Go back to your projects. I'll be back to check on you."

They were not used to her stern tone. They obeyed.

Mrs. C and Max took off running up the hill.

"Let's go see!" Sammie shouted.

"No, Sammie." Phil shook his head. "It looks serious. We

should stay out of it for now."

Sammie looked at Molly with puppy dog eyes and batted her eye scales.

Molly shook her head. "He's right, Sammie. We'll find out later. Let's get back to work."

Sammie let out a big sigh and trudged back to her clay project. But every few minutes she peeked out the window.

Max followed Mrs. C to her cabin where she prepared a thick, gooey mud pack with soothing herbs and aloe juice to suck the heat from Raif's burns.

Mr. Yuni appeared at the door with Raif in his arms.

Mrs. C pointed toward the bed. "Lay him there."

Mr. Yuni stretched Raif out on Mrs. C's bunk. He was awake, but disoriented and moaning in pain.

The burns were bright red and gooey with slimy puss oozing out. Charred black flesh reeked like fried lizard.

While Max stood wide-eyed next to her, Mrs. C knelt down and gently pressed the soothing mud mixture onto Raif's wounds. "We're lucky it missed his eyes," she whispered.

When Raif felt the cool mud on his burns he let out a loud sigh.

"Mr. Yuni, please open the medicine chest and bring the dark green syrup."

He returned in a moment, elevated Raif's head, and poured the sticky syrup in his mouth.

Raif coughed and choked.

Mr. Yuni held Raif's head up. "It's okay, son. Try to relax."

Raif gulped.

"Max, go check on the other dragons." Mr. Yuni dismissed him with a wave.

Mrs. Cleerheart gave him a compassionate look as he turned to leave.

Max trudged out of the room with a boulder of guilt on his shoulders. He had taken failure to a new level. It was bad enough that they didn't respect him. Now they weren't even safe with him.

As the magic of Mrs. C's syrup took hold, Raif relaxed and fell into a deep sleep. She pulled her stool close to his bedside and held his paw between her palms.

Mr. Yuni knelt near Raif's head and positioned his palms an inch above Raif's wounds. He took a deep breath and cleared his mind.

As he held his hands above Raif's burns, Mr. Yuni shuddered from the energy that surged through the top of his head.

Raif's eye scales fluttered.

Electricity tingled through Raif's paw into Mrs. C's hands. Her eyes popped open.

Mr. Yuni and Mrs. Cleerheart looked at each other, moved by the force that connected all of them.

Mr. Yuni's eyes filled with tears. This one is precious. I have a feeling that he is going to be healed of much more than just burns.

Chapter 20

In the days that followed, Mrs. C put Max in charge of tending Raif's wounds. She showed him how to clean the burns and apply fresh ointment to Raif's raw face.

Max read Dragon Tales when Raif was awake, and watched over him while he slept. As the pain diminished and his strength returned, they took walks together in the woods.

Max tried to apologize. "I would never have burned you on purpose, Raif. I went lizard brain before I noticed what was happening."

"You're lucky I didn't torch you back."

"I know." Max nodded. "Have you ever lost control like that?"

"No. I never cared that much about anything. But I've seen it happen in detention."

Max listened.

"Sometimes I wish I had something to get fired up about."

"But you do!"

Raif gave him a blank stare.

"You're an amazing boxer. Well, except for your footwork. You could totally win that tournament if you tried."

"Like this?" Raif pointed to his face.

Max flinched with shame. "Does it still hurt?"

"Not really. It mostly itches. But I'll never be ready in time."

Max beamed at Raif with a triumphant smile. "No, we will be ready."

After Mrs. C examined Raif's scars and gave her blessing, the pair resumed training with ferocious focus. For two weeks the Deadly Duo worked tirelessly, day and night, to prepare for the tournament.

Sometimes Sammie and Nate sneaked out of class to watch till Mr. Yuni chased them off.

As the day of the tournament drew near, Mr. Yuni warned Raif about what to expect in the ring. "Remember, these dragons are not boxing for fun. They will do anything to win. If we're lucky, we'll get a referee who is fair, but we can't count on it. The boxing business is tricky. You have to be prepared for anything – including dragons who fight dirty."

"Sounds like detention," Raif said.

Mr. Yuni nodded. "I'll do what I can to protect you, but you must see in all directions and stay fast on your feet. They'll beat you any way they can, especially if they find a vulnerable spot."

Raif drew a deep breath and tried to relax the tension in his neck.

Max chimed in. "What can I do to help?"

"You can come with us, Max. Be another pair of eyes ring-side."

Max and Raif nodded in synchrony.

"We still have a couple of days. You two, focus on footwork. I'm going to take a nap." A weary Mr. Yuni let out a sigh and trudged through the forest toward his hut. I'm getting too old for this.

Lost in thought, Mr. Yuni forgot to watch where he was stepping. His foot snagged against a root and he fell, sprawling as he tried to catch himself. He moaned as he lay on the cold ground. His twisted ankle throbbed as it swelled, and piercing pain radiated from his back to his chest.

He struggled to breathe.

He tried to relax, and focused all of his mental power on Max.

Max stopped in mid-spar. "He fell."

"Huh?"

Max pulled off his gloves, threw them to the ground, and shouted back toward Raif as he sprinted into the woods, "It's Mr. Yuni! He's hurt. Help me find him!"

Leaves crunched under dragon footfalls as Max and Raif raced toward the hut. "Mr. Yuni! Where are you?!"

No response.

They swept the area on both sides of the trail and searched behind every bush, tree, and stump.

No sign of him.

Max grew anxious.

Just then he spotted some beige fabric among the rocks. "Raif! He's over here!"

Raif ran to catch up.

"Mr. Yuni!"

No response. His eyes remained closed.

Max dropped to his knees and bent over to check their coach's pulse and respiration.

"Now what?" Raif asked.

"Let's get a board and carry him out."

"I'll go. You stay with him." Raif bounded up the hill.

Max studied Mr. Yuni's face. He had never imagined him like this. Up to now, he had seemed like a wizard – invulnerable and full of magic. What would Mr. Yuni do in a situation like this?

Max remembered how he had healed Sammie's leg. But who would heal Mr. Yuni?

Raif came scurrying down the hill, rustling through the dry leaves with a wooden door over his shoulder. Max scooted Mr. Yuni onto the board, keeping his spine and legs straight as he'd been taught during orientation week. They carefully carried Mr. Yuni up to his hut where they placed him flat on the dirt floor.

Max laid his paw on Mr. Yuni's sweaty forehead.

Raif dipped a cloth in the water pitcher and handed it to Max.

"Good idea." Max laid the cool, wet cloth across Mr. Yuni's forehead. Then he pressed it against his cheeks and throat.

Mr. Yuni let out a shallow, raspy breath. He opened his

eyes and looked up at Max.

"Mr. Yuni, where does it hurt?"

He struggled to get a breath. "B-back," he stammered in a whisper.

"Can you tell us what you need?"

"F-f-lat."

"To lie flat?"

He grunted.

Together, Max and Raif worked to carefully position Mr. Yuni. When he appeared to be more comfortable, Max asked, "Should we get Mrs. Cleerheart?"

"No."

They looked at each other. "Why?"

"No need."

"See if he wants a drink." Raif handed Max a cup of water. Max held it up to Mr. Yuni's lips.

"Ugh." He couldn't raise his head.

Raif soaked a clean cloth and drizzled water into Mr. Yuni's parched mouth.

He looked up at Raif with gratitude. Then he closed his eyes and went to sleep.

While Mr. Yuni slept, Raif ran back to camp and told Mrs.

Cleerheart what had happened, against Mr. Yuni's orders.

"Oh, yes, we've been through this before. When Mr. Yuni's back goes out, he has to lie flat for awhile."

She gave Raif a reassuring smile. "Just keep him hydrated and let him rest. I'll send some food and medicine with you. He doesn't like it when I hover." She winked.

Raif couldn't believe she trusted him with something so important. Weird.

Mrs. C filled a pack with supplies and Raif hauled it to the hut, where he and Max stayed to watch over their teacher.

Mrs. C went about her business with her usual calm, so the remaining dragons figured that everything was going to be okay.

That evening, she called a community meeting in the dining hall and brought her tribal talking stick made from a painted gourd and firebird feathers.

"Tonight we're going to give each other feedback about our progress." Mrs. C placed a chair in the middle of the circle. "Each of you will take a turn."

The dragons looked at each other. Molly gulped.

"How do we know if we've made progress?" Sammie asked.

"Good question, Sammie. Remember, the first week of camp, when we set goals for change?"

They all nodded.

"Well, now that we've been here a few weeks, let's review our goals and see how far we've come. Who would like to go first?"

"I will." Molly volunteered in her tiny voice and sat down in the feedback chair. She couldn't wait to get it over with.

"Thank you, Molly. Please tell us why you came to Dragon Camp."

"Well, I missed a lot of school. And I was afraid of almost everything. Sometimes I just stayed in bed." Her cheeks turned a deeper pink.

"Thank you. Now who would like to give feedback to Molly?'

"I will! I will!" Sammie's paw shot up high in the air and she bounced in her chair.

Mrs. C handed the talking stick to Sammie who grabbed it with gusto.

"Molly, I think you are making really good progress at camp because you always go to class and you never stay in bed except for that first day, and also you tumped Raif in Aikido class."

The other dragons laughed.

Mrs. C smiled. "Very good, Sammie. Anything else?"

"Oh yeah, and you are a really good painter."

Molly blushed.

"Okay, who's next?"

Silence. Tension.

A loud dragon fart ripped out from under Nate's tail and the smell of dead fish filled the room.

"Eww!" Sammie yelled and ran outside, waving her paw in front of her nose. "Jeez, Nate, what did you eat?"

The other dragons moved toward the open window.

Nate cackled.

Mrs. C rapped her bamboo stick on the charcoal board. "Back to the circle, please. Who's next?"

"I'll go," said Phil.

Sammie started to pass the talking stick to him but tickled his belly with the feathers instead.

Phil giggled. "I agree with Sammie, and I also think you are a very nice person." Phil's cheeks turned pink against his will. "But what did you mean by fears?"

"Um...well...like I was talking to Max about how I was afraid to go to art school, and he talked to me and helped me stop being afraid."

Phil felt a pang of jealousy in his gut. "Oh."

"And I was afraid to go to Aikido class, but then Mr. Yuni

showed me how to take down Raif."

"Yeah!" Sammie yelled.

"But then I was afraid I hurt him." Molly scrunched her face scales.

After Molly received her feedback, the other three followed. Nate explained how he'd been sent to camp for his hot temper, and how Max had shown him the Dragon Thermometer and taught him to use his breath to keep cool.

Phil talked about how he used to get in trouble when he disappeared at school. He told them about the day Max followed him into the woods and drew a portrait of him instead of yelling at him. "That was really cool, but don't say anything to Max. He doesn't know I saw him."

They all nodded.

Sammie went last. "They told me I had to go to camp because I was impulsive."

"What's that?" Nate asked.

"Well, one day I got bored and ran around the school naked."

They all burst into raucous laughter.

"And another time they punished me for something stupid so I climbed up on the roof and threatened to jump off."

"Maybe you just have big feelings," Molly said. Molly was suddenly in her comfort zone: taking care of someone else like she did with her mom at home.

"She has big feelings about Raif!" Nate blurted out.

The dragons laughed.

Sammie fumed. "Shut up, Nate!" She hopped up and socked him on the wing.

"Ow!" He whirled his tail around and farted on her.

"Gross!"

Nate giggled and pointed at her.

"Please sit down," said Mrs. C. "Go on, Molly."

"It's good to have big feelings," Molly said. "Maybe all you need is a pause button."

"What's that?" Sammie examined her paws.

The group laughed.

"The other kind of pause, Sammie." Molly explained in her gentle way. "Like a stop sign – something that reminds you to stop and think before you act."

"Think about what?" Sammie asked.

"Oh, like if you might get in trouble. Or if someone could get hurt."

"Hmm." Sammie crinkled her nose scales.

"You can still do what you want, but if you pause and think

first, you have more control over yourself."

"How do you know about that?" Sammie asked.

"Umm..." Molly's cheeks turned deep pink. "My feelings used to get out of control."

"Really?"

Molly nodded and pulled a silver medallion out from under her t-shirt. It had a big yellow star in the center, engraved with four letters.

Sammie read it out loud, "S.T.A.R. What does it mean?

"Stop... Think... Act... Reflect."

"Cool!" Sammie fondled the medallion.

"That little star keeps me out of trouble sometimes."

Sammie gave her a curious look.

So did Phil.

"Okay, everyone, it's time to wrap up." Mrs. C said. "Sammie, before we stop, is there anything we can do to help you with your goals?"

"Remind me to pause?"

"Very good." Mrs. C smiled. "And how would you like us to do that?"

Sammie grinned, shoved both of her stubby paws out in front of her face, and shouted, "Paws!"

They all laughed.

Chapter 21

Max and Raif camped out near Mr. Yuni's hut that night and watched over him while he slept. He slept and slept like a hybernating bear and did not move till morning.

Max rose early and built a fire for cooking breakfast. He prepared the calming chamomile tea that Mrs. C had sent and hoped Mr. Yuni would be able to drink it.

Just as the tea was ready to serve, Mr. Yuni stirred. "Max?"

Max heard his name from inside the hut and hurried to Mr. Yuni's side. "Good morning. How are you feeling?"

"I'm starving."

Max grinned. He turned around to see Raif standing in the doorway. "He's hungry."

Raif smiled and prepared breakfast.

"What day is it?" Mr. Yuni asked.

"It's Friday."

"Friday? That means the tournament is tomorrow!"

Max patted Mr. Yuni's shoulder and held a cup of tea to his lips.

Mr. Yuni raised his head just a little, with Max's help, and took a sip. He stared at Max. "You must go."

Raif returned with some fish cakes. "Go where?"

"The tournament."

Raif shook his head. "Not without you." His horns twitched. "I'd get creamed. Cream of Dragon Soup."

"No, you must. It is your time. Max will coach you."

Max and Raif looked at each other with wide eyes. "Huh?" They asked in harmony.

"Max, can you drive?" Mr. Yuni asked.

"Uh, yeah..."

"Good. Take my truck. I registered both of you. You don't need me there."

Max gulped.

"But who will take care of you?" Raif asked. "You can't even get up."

"Tell Mrs. Cleerheart to send Nate with some food and water. You two need to get ready for the tournament. Review your strategy, do some yoga, and get plenty of sleep tonight. You will need it."

Max and Raif hung around while Mr. Yuni finished his breakfast. When they tried to linger, he shooed them away. "Get going, you two. I'll be fine."

"Okay. We'll send Nate."

"Good luck, Raif. You will do well. Remember: the best defense is to not be there."

"Thank you, sir."

"And good luck to you, Coach Max." Mr. Yuni winked.

Max just stared.

The nervous pair quickly kicked some dirt on the fire and hurried back to camp.

Mr. Yuni lay flat and tried to relax his back.

But, after a few minutes, a startling scent wafted in on the breeze and made him tense up again.

Smoke.

Max and Raif returned to camp and explained the situation to Mrs. C who took it in stride and helped them get ready for the tournament. They reviewed strategy while Nate hiked out to Mr. Yuni's hut with supplies.

Finally, I get to do something besides sit in class! Nate skipped through dry leaves and kicked rocks off the path as he made his way through the woods. It felt so good to be out on his own for a change. He whistled a tune and didn't even notice the weight of the pack on his back.

As he neared Mr. Yuni's hut, his song was interrupted by a muffled shout.

"Help!"

He took off running.

Black smoke filled the air in front of Mr. Yuni's hut, and flames licked at the doorframe.

Oh no.

Fire blocked the entrance, so he ran around back and searched for another way in. Frantic, he tried to pry his way through the wall of the hut with his claws.

Too thick.

He looked up.

In a flash of superdragon strength, Nate sprang up into the air and clamped onto the roof. He attacked the bamboo with his claws and ripped a hole.

Nate dropped down through the opening into the smoke-filled hut and waved the black poison away from his face.

Mr. Yuni gasped and choked as he struggled to get up.

"Mr. Yuni, what should I do?"

"Suffocate the flames." He pointed to a stack of old wool blankets.

Nate seized the heavy pile in a powerful bear hug and hefted them over to where the fire had begun to devour the doorframe and creep up toward the dry, thatched roof.

With all of his fury, Nate assaulted the flames with a heavy blanket. He pounded away, up and down the doorframe, until the last bit of fire was snuffed out. Then he grabbed the cor-

ners of Mr. Yuni's blanket and dragged him through the ashes into the open air.

Mr. Yuni coughed and coughed.

Nate scurried behind the hut and found his pack where he had dropped it. He pulled out a bottle of water, and Mr. Yuni gulped it down as if his throat were parched.

Nate's face scales were blackened by smoke, and his eyes burned red.

"You... saved...my life." Mr. Yuni's dark brown eyes glistened with gratitude.

Nate gulped. It was such a weird feeling – an adult saying he'd done something right. Usually adults only talked to him when he was in trouble.

He and Mr. Yuni breathed in the fresh air until they both calmed down.

"How did the fire start?" Nate asked.

"Looks like our morning campfire got out of control." He motioned toward the trail of ashes.

Nate raised his eyebrow scales.

"Let's have a look in that pack and see what Mrs. Cleerheart sent us for lunch." Mr. Yuni winked.

Nate used one of the blankets as a tablecloth and spread out a picnic of vegetables, salmon jerky, and dragonberry pie.

"Help me sit up." Mr. Yuni motioned for Nate to prop him up against a scorchbark tree. He grunted with pain as he moved.

Nate froze. "Am I hurting you?"

"No, I'm just sore."

The two sat together in the cool shade and recovered from their ordeal in silence.

After awhile, Mr. Yuni asked, "How do you like camp so far?"

"It's okay. I like the skateboard ramp."

"You did a really nice job with that, Nate. Would you like to try another woodworking project?"

"I dunno."

"We still have a few weeks left."

Nate looked up and pointed to Mr. Yuni's scorched hut. "How 'bout that?"

Mr. Yuni strained to look. "Oh my."

His beloved golden hut looked like the head of a devouring death god with its huge, black, gaping mouth.

"Maybe we could fix it up. Make it better than before."

Mr. Yuni smiled. "That would be wonderful, Nate."

"We could make a window in case you ever need to get out."

Mr. Yuni pointed to the hole in the roof. "Like that one?" He grinned.

Nate tensed up, worried that he was in trouble.

"You must be very strong."

"That's what they said at school. I'm s'posed to use my strength for good instead of fighting."

"Well, you certainly did that today. You like to fight?"

Nate gave him a fangy grin and nodded.

"Maybe I can teach you some Kung Fu when I'm on my feet again."

"Really?!" Nate hopped to his paws with a huge grin.

"It's the least I can do. Just promise me that you won't get into any more fights at school, okay?"

Nate nodded so fast his horns hurt.

"If you work hard and stay out of trouble, maybe you can train for the martial arts tournament next year. They have a junior division, you know."

"Really?" Nate's tail flicked.

"Yes, sir. Right alongside the big boys."

"Wow." Nate gazed off into the distance. He'd always imagined a skateboarding trophy above his fireplace, but now he could see a black belt hanging right next to it.

Chapter 22

The next morning Max and Raif rose early and packed the truck. Mrs. C prepared lunch and plenty of snacks for the trip, and filled some canteens with water. She sent along first-aid supplies and pain medicine, just in case – no predicting what might happen at these dragon events.

Max spread a tarp over the supplies and tied it to the truck bed, then went inside to eat breakfast.

Sammie wiggled and fidgeted more than usual that morning.

"What's with you, girl? You got fire ants in your pants?" Raif winked at her.

Sammie ignored him and scarfed down her fish cakes.

After breakfast, they cleaned up, and the younger dragons went to arts and crafts while Max and Raif headed out for the tournament. Mrs. Cleerheart stood and waved as they drove off down the dusty road.

When she returned to the studio, she found two quiet dragons working on their projects: Molly stood at the easel, brush in hand, while Phil constructed a colorful fabric cover for his book.

Mrs. C looked around outside, then hurried back in. "Has

anyone seen Sammie?"

They looked up from their work.

"She was at breakfast," Molly said.

"And she helped clean up," Phil added.

"Uh-oh..." Molly scrunched up her forehead scales.

"What is it, Molly?" Mrs. C asked.

"Did Max and Raif leave yet?"

"Yes, I saw them off about ten minutes ago."

"She was dying to go to that tournament with Raif." She gave Mrs. C a knowing look.

"Oh my." Mrs. C pursed her lips and widened her eyes. "Good thing I packed extra fish cakes."

Chapter 23

"Ow!"

"What was that?" Max asked. He thought he heard a yelp from the truck bed when he hit a bump in the road.

Raif popped up out of his seat and stretched his long torso out the window to peer under the tarp.

Sammie's green eyes sparkled at him. "Shhh!" She slapped her scaly index finger over her lips.

Raif chuckled. "You crazy little monkey. What are you doing back there?"

Max's horns twitched.

Raif sat back down. "We've got a stowaway. Guess who."

Max turned and looked at Raif's grin. "No way."

"Way. And it's too late to turn back. Looks like we have a fan club."

"Can we keep her safe at the tournament?"

"Yeah, she's a scrappy one."

"Do you want to bring her up front?" Max asked.

"Nah, let her bounce around back there for awhile. She'll get tired of it."

A few minutes later Raif heard a tap tap tap behind him and saw Sammie's horns sticking up. "I have to go to the bathroom!" she shouted above the rattling of the truck.

When the trio arrived at the tournament, they could not believe their eyes. Hundreds of dragons of all shapes, sizes, and colors, swarmed around a nucleus of six boxing rings – one for each division.

Raif gulped.

"Let's stick close together so we don't get separated," Max said.

"Good idea." Raif nodded.

Sammie gawked at the spectacle.

As the band of three drew near the crowd, they could barely hear each other above the cacophony.

Max shouted, "Look for a sign that says Y.A."

"What's that?" Sammie asked.

"Young Adult Division. That's Raif's age classification."

Sammie looked around. "There it is!" She pointed and took off toward the sign.

"Whoa, little one." Raif grabbed her shoulder and dragged her back. "Let's stick together. If you get lost here, we'll never find you."

Max kept an eye on Sammie while Raif checked in and looked at the schedule.

"We have an hour before my first fight," Raif told them. "I need to warm up."

Sammie foraged for snacks and Max practiced his yoga breathing while Raif stretched.

"I'm gonna hurl." Raif's purple face scales turned a little green.

"That's normal. It'll pass. Just remember what Mr. Yuni said: take deep breaths and focus on what is in front of you."

Raif tried to inhale deeper.

"You've done this a hundred times before, Raif, and those dragons in detention were tough."

"Yeah." Raif tried again to breathe but his anxiety got in the way.

Max punched him in the stomach.

"Hey!" Raif scowled at him.

"Now you're not nervous. Now you're mad."

Chapter 24

Raif and Max stood together in the corner of the ring and waited for the bell. Max clamped his paws onto Raif's muscular shoulders and stared into his eyes. "Remember: side to side, stick and move. The best defense is to not be there."

Raif nodded.

"And remember to breathe or I'll sock you again."

The deafening clang of the bell jarred them. "Attention! Attention! Contestants to the center of the ring!"

Max climbed out through the ropes and stood next to Sammie.

Raif strutted to the center and faced a fierce-looking yellow dragon named Lurch who stood almost a head taller than him.

"Wow, that guy's big!" Sammie said.

"Yeah, but Raif's fast." Max tried to stop fidgeting.

Raif looked up at Lurch and gave him the stink eye.

"I'm gonna squish you like a little bug." Lurch bared his fangs.

"You're gonna have to catch me first." Raif gave him an icy stare.

As he waited for the bell, Raif flashed back to detention – his cold, dark cell, back before Max and Sammie and Mr. Yuni.

His stomach clenched when he remembered the first time he fought one of the big guys. They were mean.

But Raif was smart.

The bell clanged.

Raif landed a right jab to Lurch's jaw and darted out of reach.

Lurch looked as if he'd been rudely awakened from a nap. He roared, swung at Raif's head, and missed.

Raif taunted. "Catch me if you can, T. Rex!" He danced around with a self-satisfied smirk on his handsome face.

"Ha! He showed him!" Sammie shouted. "Go Raif!"

Max hyper-focused on Raif's moves. "Side to side, Raif. Stick him."

Raif landed another jab to the jaw followed by a hook to the midsection.

Max couldn't believe it. Was this the same dragon who could barely move his feet a couple months ago? That Mr. Yuni was a miracle worker. I wonder how Mr. Yuni is doing. I'll bet he's bummed he can't be here.

SMACK! Lurch popped Raif in the jaw.

Raif stumbled backward, almost lost his balance, then found his feet again.

Lurch slapped Raif's horns. "You're not so hard to catch, Shortie."

Raif's temperature rose. His nostrils burned, his horns spiked straight up. His powerful tail whipped from side to side as he attacked.

With the frustrated fury of a caged bird, he tore into Lurch's face and midsection. Left, right, left, right, blow after blow, like a woodpecker boring into a scorchbark tree.

And, like a tree, Lurch fell, with a gigantic thud in the middle of the ring. He did not get up.

Sammie went berserk screaming and cheering. She bounded over the ropes and flung herself into Raif's sweaty torso.

Max peeled her off. "Sammie, you have to stay outside the ring." He lifted her over the top rope and planted her back where she belonged.

Dazed, Raif stood in the middle of the ring and stared at the pile of yellow on the floor in disbelief.

Max grabbed Raif's gloved paw and held it high in the air.

The crowd cheered and chanted, "Raif! Raif! Raif! Raif!"

Sammie jumped up and down, giggling.

Max led the disoriented warrior to the corner of the ring and checked his eyes and face. "That was amazing," Max said.

Raif grunted.

Word of the ferocious fight spread through the crowd like a swarm of fire wasps. With each successive victory throughout the day, Raif's adoring audience grew. Their chanting grew louder and more frenzied.

A few hours later, he had reached the semi-finals. Only two more fights and it would be over. He was glad, because he was getting tired.

As he grew more fatigued, it became harder to "not be there," as Mr. Yuni had taught him. His footwork slowed and became sloppy, and his biceps burned from holding his gloved paws up all day long.

In the last round of the semi-finals, a big blue dragon cut Raif's left eye before he could get out of the way.

And before Raif knocked him out.

One final opponent remained: an ugly, red dragon from wilderness camp. He looked familiar, but Raif couldn't place him. He had those creepy, cold eyes like a snake, and his square face was covered with scars. He looked as if he'd been attacked by a razor hedge.

"This is it, Raif. Just one more and we're home." Max smeared Mrs. C's ointment on Raif's injured eye. "Remember the basics: side to side, stick and move."

Raif nodded. His eye throbbed and gave him a headache.

"Can you see?" Max examined the cut.

"It's kind of blurry," Raif said. "It feels like he left one of his claws in my eye."

Max shuddered. "Well, keep it covered. If it gets too bad,

I'll stop the fight." Max wiped away the excess ointment.

Raif seized Max's wrist. "No. I'm going to finish it."

Raif's intensity startled Max and scared him. "Uh..well... keep it covered then. Don't lose your eye over a stupid fight."

Raif pounded his gloves together and stood up. He shook out his arms, jumped up and down a few times, and looked for his opponent.

Ugly Red stood in the center of the ring grinning at Raif. His eyes were a weird yellow color, like squash, and he was missing a fang right in front.

"Well, well, well. If it isn't little baby Raifie." The red dragon snorted and chuckled.

Raif strained his memory to place the familiar voice. Oh no. In a flash, it all came back. This was Needles. Raif hadn't seen him in years. He hardly recognized his scarred up face.

But he could never forget that name. Nor the day when that horrible reptile was finally kicked out of detention and sent to wilderness camp for mutilating his opponent's face.

With needles.

The butterflies in Raif's stomach turned into pterodactyls. He remembered Mr. Yuni's warning about dragons fighting dirty.

That was the only way Needles fought.

I can't believe they let him into the tournament. Mr. Yuni wasn't kidding when he said the boxing business is tricky.

"Hey, bud," Max said. "You okay?"

"Yeah."

"What is it?"

"I know him from detention."

Max looked Needles up and down.

"What do you know about him?"

"He cheats. And he likes to inflict pain."

Max bugged his eyes out.

"See his face?"

Max looked. "Eww."

"Yeah. That's what happens when cheaters fight cheaters. They all end up mangled."

"What's going on?" Sammie leaned way over and tried to eavesdrop.

Max waved her away. "Go back to your spot."

Sammie scowled and stomped back to her place outside the ring.

Max grabbed Raif's shoulder, staring into his eyes. "Don't take any chances. It's not worth it."

Raif grunted and glared at Needles.

"Fighters into the ring!" The ref shouted.

The opponents stalked to the center of the ring and glowered at each other.

Raif's cool blue eyes turned to ice. He remembered his first year in detention. He had a friend named Joey. They were the youngest dragons on cellblock A.

But Joey was not a fighter. Needles and his gang beat Joey to dragonfruit pulp and stole his toys. Then they stole his blanket. They kept on until his cell was bare.

When Joey couldn't take it anymore, he escaped into the wilderness. Raif never saw him again, and he never found another friend.

The starting bell jerked Raif back into the present moment. A giant fist slammed into his cheekbone. He spun around.

Fueled by past fury, Raif plowed his fist into Needles' scarred up face with a loud SMACK!

Raif roared. So did his fans.

Needles bugged his eyes and shook out his face scales.

The fatigue of the day dissolved. Super-charged adrenaline took over. Raif hammered Needles' head over and over, trying to knock it off.

The crowd erupted with a big racket. They breathed flames and smoke up into the sky.

Needles delivered a vicious blow to Raif's injured eye.

"No!" Sammie shouted.

The crowd booed, except for a few hecklers who laughed and cheered.

Raif blocked his face with both gloves. Needles went after his midsection. He pounded on the same spot over and over till something cracked inside. Raif felt a piercing pain. He yowled.

"Raif!" Max panicked. He tried to catch his breath.

The bell clanged. Round one was over.

Raif sank onto his stool in the corner. Max cleaned up his eye, and plastered tape over his ribs.

"Raif, listen to me. If you focus on your injuries, you won't be able to fight."

Raif grunted.

"Remember what Mr. Yuni said: Don't be there. You have to keep dancing and dancing, just like we did on the dock. Let him wear himself out punching air."

Raif listened.

"And when he gets tired, smash his ugly face in."

Raif grinned.

"This is it, buddy. You're gonna have to move faster than you have ever moved in your life. And keep it going till you knock him out."

Raif stood and smacked his gloves together.

"Get him, Raif!" Sammie shouted.

Raif pulled the strings on his gloves tighter with his teeth. A dragonfly zipped past his ear and got up in his face like Mr. Yuni sometimes did. It disappeared as quickly as it arrived, then it reappeared, like magic, right in front of his nose.

A strange sense of peace calmed Raif's heart.

He took a deep breath and strode to the center of the ring for round two.

Something happened to Raif between rounds one and two. He got it.

Needles swung. Raif disappeared, then popped up, surprising his opponent with a jab.

Again and again, Raif disappeared then reappeared to throw a sting.

Needles' face contorted with rage. After several rounds of boxing air, he stomped to the corner, grabbed his coach by the collar, and pulled him out of the ring.

Sammie smelled trouble. She sneaked away to spy on Needles.

Hidden behind the ring, his coach crouched down and

wove a razor hedge thorn into the seam of Needles' glove. It was the same color as the leather, but Sammie saw it sticking out from the part of the glove that would hit Raif's eye.

Sammie gasped and ran back to Max. She tried to climb into the ring to tell Raif.

Max pulled her back. "Where have you been?"

"He's cheating!" Sammie yelled into Max's ear.

"Who's cheating?"

"Needles put a big sticker in his glove to poke Raif!"

"Oh no...!" Max clenched up all over.

Raif moved to the center of the ring and tightened his gloves.

"Raif!" Max shouted, but the clang of the bell and the roaring crowd drowned him out.

Needles gave Raif an evil grin. Swung at his eye.

Raif ducked.

Rotton squash-colored eyes blazing, Needles went after Raif's injured eye like a hungry honey badger.

Max felt fire rise behind his nostrils.

"Ahh!" Raif screamed in pain as Needles landed a jab below his eye that punctured the skin. Blood streamed down Raif's face scales, dripped on the floor.

"Cheater!" Sammie bounded over the top rope and charged.

She launched into the air with a war whoop. Her feet slammed into Needles' chest. She dug her claws into his sweaty, smelly scales.

He yowled in pain and fell flat on his back. The floor shook.

Sammie sat on Needles' chest and yanked off his glove. "Look, Raif. He was going to put your eye out." She tossed the glove to Raif and spat in Needles' face.

The referee shouted, "Get out!" and pointed to Sammie's spot outside the ropes.

She gave him the stink eye and stomped away with her paws on her hips.

The ref grabbed the glove from Raif and examined it.

Raif pointed to the thorn. "They don't call him Needles for nuthin'."

"I guess not." The ref ripped the thorn out of the glove and hurled it at Needles' coach. He examined Raif's injuries. "You okay?"

"Yeah," Raif said.

"I can disqualify him, or you can fight him."

"I want to finish it."

The ref nodded, gave Needles time to pull on a new glove, then motioned for the bout to continue.

Needles hoisted himself up off the floor and stood, a little unsteady.

Raif danced from foot to foot. "C'mon!" He waved Needles to the center of the ring.

Needles winced.

Throughout the remaining rounds of the fight, Raif moved faster than he'd ever moved in his life. By the last round, Needles sagged with exhaustion. When Raif knocked him down, he stayed down.

The ref counted to ten, then hoisted Raif's arm.

A big red pile of reptile on the mat moaned and closed its eyes.

The crowd exploded with cheers and chanted, "Raif! Raif! Raif! Raif!" They shot flames up into the air and stormed the ring in a cloud of multi-colored smoke. Raif's fans hoisted him onto their shoulders and paraded him around.

With a weary smile, Raif pointed at Sammie.

Sammie squealed with delight as a mob of dragons scooped her up and marched her around alongside her beloved Raif.

Chapter 25

When the triumphant trio arrived back at camp, they were too tired to talk. Well, except for Sammie. She could keep talking as long as anyone was awake enough to listen. Molly hung in there as long as she could, but eventually fell asleep in her chair.

Mrs. Cleerheart served them some drowsy dragon tea, and they slept like three big river rocks.

When they finally woke up late Sunday morning, Nate and

Mr. Yuni had just returned from the woods. Mr. Yuni limped along with a walking stick and had a hard time getting in and out of his chair, but he was happy to be on his feet again.

Phil and Molly were just back from the woods too. He had shown her his secret hideaway illuminated by the colors of the sunrise. Of all the campers, only she could really appreciate it.

When the cozy pair appeared, paw in paw, Nate pointed at them and made loud smooching sounds. Their face scales turned deep red, and they sat down at opposite ends of the dining room.

Everyone huddled around the brunch table, mouths watering at the sweet aroma of Mrs. C's dragonberry pancakes. They listened to each others' stories: Mr. Yuni's tumble in the woods, Nate's fire fighting adventure, Raif's stowaway fan club, and, of course, Sammie's daring feats at the tournament. In her mind, she was the hero of the day.

Raif watched Sammie with fond eyes while she embellished her tale.

"So, Raif, how does it feel to be a champion?" Mr. Yuni asked.

"Surreal." Raif gave him a quizzical look. His face was swollen, and the scales around his eye had turned purple and blue overnight.

"He was incredible," Max said, "absolutely fearless and quick as a hornet bird."

"I had a good coach," Raif mumbled through his pancakes.

Max nodded. "That's right, Mr. Yuni. You did an amazing job training Raif."

"I meant you," Raif said.

Max blushed.

"What about me?" Sammie yelled with her mouth full, and a blob of her chewed up pancakes spewed onto Nate.

"Hey!" Nate wiped the sticky slime off his scales.

Raif chuckled. "Oh, yeah. We can't forget the crazy little monkey who saved me from Old Needle Face."

They all laughed, and lingered long around the table that morning, talking and teasing.

Like a big, noisy family.

Chapter 26

During the remaining weeks of camp, Max worked closely with each dragon to help them achieve their summer goals. He had the brilliant idea to pair up Molly and Sammie so they could influence each other. Molly learned Sammie's fearlessness while Sammie modeled Molly's self-control.

One morning Molly surprised her young friend with a mini-spa day of dragonberry smoothies and an aromatherapy facial. Sammie peeled the cucumbers off her eyes scales and munched on them.

Phil spent hours in his tree every day working on his story while Mr. Yuni showed Nate how to repair the hut and taught him Kung Fu moves.

Max carved out as much time as he could to work on portraits. When the dragons weren't looking, he stayed busy capturing each of them in their element.

As part of his application to art school, Max wrote an essay about his summer at Dragon Camp.

I believe the lessons I've learned as a camp counselor will serve me well as an art student. At the beginning of the summer, I was full of fear and self-doubt. Every time I made a mistake, I would beat myself up and think about going home.

But I discovered that mistakes are how we learn, and that I can be my own best friend by being gentle with myself when I fail. I've learned that if I really believe in myself, anything is possible.

When Max read his completed essay, he was amazed at how much he had changed in only three months. He thought back to when his change had started. When he realized that Mr. Yuni and Mrs. C believed in him, he'd started to believe in himself.

No one knew what Raif's summer goals were. He'd sort of gotten a pass when he won the tournament, and the others assumed that's what he was aiming for. But Raif knew.

He wanted to fly.

So, when the other dragons were busy, Raif sneaked off to the waterfall and tested his wings, more carefully now, so he wouldn't become a big, scaly rock formation at the bottom of the river.

Each day he soared a little higher and traveled a little farther. As his skills improved, his confidence grew.

One day he flew across the river, over the falls, and into the wilderness, toward the green mountains.

Meanwhile, summer was almost over and it was time to make plans for the fall. Some dragons would return to their classrooms for a second chance while others would go on to new schools for a fresh start.

Max hoped to go to art school, but he hadn't heard any news. If they liked his essay, he might get an interview where he could show his paintings.

Day after day he watched the mailbox and worked hard to perfect his portraits.

He tried not to get his hopes too high, thinking, oh well, even if I don't get in, we'll have some art for the dining hall.

One afternoon during rec, a car pulled up at the gate. Raif spun around to see if it was his probation officer. He had almost forgotten that he would have to return to the depressing grey of cellblock A.

A woman and a man, both in fancy suits, climbed out of the car.

They walked up to Mr. Yuni and smiled. The woman spoke. "Excuse me sir, we are from the Dragon Institute of Fine Arts. We were visiting a student nearby, and thought we'd stop by and meet Max. Would that be all right?"

Max jumped up from the dirt where he'd been wrestling with Nate. He brushed off his dusty scales and hurried to greet his guests. "Hi, I'm Max." He wiped his paw and reached out for a handshake.

"Hello, Max, it's very nice to met you." The woman gave him a curious look. "We were enchanted by your essay and wanted to see the camp."

Max gulped.

"Would you like a tour?" Mr. Yuni asked.

"That would be lovely."

Max led them around the grounds, and Mrs. C showed them the art studio. "Would you like something cold to drink?" She asked the visitors. It was a hot day.

They nodded with enthusiasm. "Yes, please."

Mrs. C led Max and the visitors into the dining hall for some cold dragonflower tea.

But she wasn't really there for the tea. "Max, why don't you show our visitors the portraits you've been working on."

Max's stomach clenched. This was it – the moment he'd been waiting for. And dreading.

"They're over here." Max motioned toward the gallery. At the top of the wall hung a sign that Mr. Yuni had carved in calligraphy: Dragons In Their Element.

The couple stared at the intricate images of Phil writing in his forest hideout, Molly painting fire lilies, Mr. Yuni meditating in front of his hut, Sammie and Nate flying through the air on their skateboards...

"Wow," they exclaimed in unison. "These are fantastic."

"I still have a couple more to finish," Max said. "There's Mrs. Cleerheart in her garden and Raif in his boxing gloves."

The man spoke. "Max, we were impressed by your essay, but we had no idea that you could paint like this."

The woman stepped forward. "Max, I can't say this official-ly yet, but welcome to the Dragon Arts Academy."

Max's eyes bugged out. His heart raced, and a gigantic grin lit up his face.

Chapter 27

That evening at dinner celebration filled the air. Max was as high as a pterodactyl in flight.

So was Molly. The possibility of art school had opened up a whole new world for her. If Max could make his dreams come true, maybe she could too.

But a cold, grey cloud hung over Raif as he sat quietly on the edge of the party. It hadn't been his P.O. at the gate today, but it soon would be. In a couple of weeks, the detention truck would come to take him back to his cell. His home, he supposed. He didn't have anywhere else to go.

A strange sensation rose in Raif's throat and welled up behind his eyes – an emotion he hadn't felt in a long time.

Mrs. Cleerheart saw his pain. "Raif, would you help me with the dessert please?"

"Okay."

He shuffled after her into the kitchen.

She laid a gentle hand on his shoulder and looked into his sad eyes. "Raif, your sorrow wants to be released."

He crinkled his forehead scales.

"I know you had to be tough for a long time. You had to survive. But now you are safe. It's time to heal."

Raif stared at her. "How can you tell?"

Mrs. Cleerheart drew a deep breath. "Because I've been there, my dear."

Raif cocked his head to the side. His horns jiggled. He found it hard to believe this sweet old lady had anything in common with him.

"Are you ready to get rid of that pain?"

He nodded.

Mrs. C closed the kitchen door and they stood together in the fading light.

Raif's blue eyes flooded with tears. His grief had waited a long time to find a home, and it was not going to wait one minute longer.

Mrs. C placed her palm over his heart. "Breathe, my dear. And when you exhale, let it go. Release it and let it go on its way."

Fire flashed from Raif's nostrils as he exhaled. Then he exploded with convulsing sobs that turned his flames to steam. A lifetime of stored up emotion gushed down his face and made trails of mud all over his dusty scales. He clutched Mrs. C in a tight hug and wept on her shoulder till her blouse was soaked.

She held him and patted his back. "It's okay. You're home now."

Raif's ears spiked up. Home?

When he was all cried out, Mrs. C handed him a face towel. "You've very brave, my dear. Mourning is hard work."

Raif flushed. "This has never happened before."

"When you let go of that old pain, you create space for something new. Space that you can fill with whatever you want."

Raif gave her a curious look.

Later that night, while the dragons slept, Mr. Yuni and Mrs. Cleerheart sat outside by the fire.

"I have a favor to ask," Mrs. C said.

Mr. Yuni looked up at her and grinned. "Does this favor involve a certain boxing champ?"

Chapter 28

When Raif woke up the next morning, his throat was parched and his head hurt from sobbing. Mrs. C was right. Letting go was hard work.

Did I actually cry like a little baby just because some old lady told me to?

Raif believed he had reached a dead end. He could either go back to detention, or he could fly away over the river and disappear. Maybe he could survive in the mountains on his own.

Either way, this crying business made no sense. He had to stay tough for detention, but if he flew away, he sure wasn't going with his guts hanging out.

Tormented by a splitting headache and a dark mood, Raif stomped to the kitchen to get some water for his burning throat. When he returned, he found Mr. Yuni waiting outside his cabin.

"Did you sleep well?"

Raif grunted.

"Do you have time for a hike before breakfast?"

"Okay." Raif wanted to go back to bed, but he decided to humor the old man. He had taught him to box after all.

They tromped through a wet forest, fragrant with dragon blossoms, and warmed by the orange sunrise. A chorus of birds chattered their excitement about the new day. Raif plowed through branches without bothering to duck, and dew-soaked leaves slapped his face scales.

"Raif, I have a favor to ask of you. You are under no obligation, of course, but I would like you to consider it."

Raif grunted and kept walking.

"I need someone to help me here at the campground after the dragons leave. We have many repairs to do, and upkeep of the grounds. I'm getting too old to do it all myself."

Raif raised his eyebrow scales and looked over at Mr. Yuni.

"We would pay you a salary, of course, and your meals would be free. You could have your choice of the cabins, or we could build you a hut in the woods if you prefer."

Raif's mind reeled. Wait a minute...am I dreaming? Did I go back to bed?

"Oh, and Mrs. Cleerheart can tutor you if you would like to complete your schooling."

Raif squinted his eyes into suspicious slits. He examined Mr. Yuni's expression. Why would he pick me? "What about my P.O.?" Raif asked. "He's coming to take me back to detention."

"Son, why do you believe you came here this summer?"

158

"I don't know. Punishment, I guess."

"Your P.O. tells me you have a good heart. He wants you to have a chance for a better life."

Raif squirmed.

"This is your chance."

"What about Max?" Raif asked. "Doesn't he want the job?"

"Max is going to art school."

Raif nodded and tried to let it all sink in. They walked on in silence for awhile.

"You hungry?" Mr. Yuni asked.

"Yeah."

"Let's get some breakfast."

Raif had a new experience as he sat among his friends at breakfast. His heart felt full.

Mrs. C clinked her spoon against a cup. "Attention please. I have an announcement."

The chattering dragons grew still and listened.

"We're having a graduation ceremony next weekend to honor all of you and to celebrate your accomplishments. I need volunteers to help with set up, decorations, and entertainment."

"Sammie and I can decorate," Molly said.

"Yeah!" Sammie grinned.

"I'll help you set up," said Nate.

"Terrific. Thank you." Mrs. C nodded. "And what about entertainment?"

No one spoke. They all looked around at each other.

"Well, I have something entertaining." Raif smirked. "But it's at the very end."

"What is it?" Sammie popped up out of her chair.

"It's a surprise." Raif winked at her.

They all grew quiet again.

"Umm..." Phil cleared his throat. "Would a story count as entertainment?"

Everyone looked at Phil.

"Yes, Phil, a story would be perfect." Mrs. C gave him an encouraging smile.

Phil shuffled out of the dining hall and disappeared.

"He's weird." Sammie whispered to Molly.

Molly smiled. "He's an artist."

In the days that followed, Nate sawed and hammered and built a graduation platform while Molly painted a banner, and Sammie created colorful decorations.

Phil hid out in his tree and worked furiously to finish his story on time.

Max and Mr. Yuni cleaned up the grounds and repaired some of the old benches that had grown wobbly and splintery over time.

Raif helped a little here and there, but he was obsessed with flying. One day he flew far past the river and disappeared for hours. No one saw him till after dark.

Chapter 29

Finally Graduation Day arrived, clear and sunny with a cool breeze that made everything feel perfect. Black and yellow butterflies flitted against the blue sky. Tree tops whished in the wind.

A chorus of birds sang out their joyful accompaniment, and bright blue dragonflies danced above the lake.

A mouth-watering combination of luscious aromas wafted on the breeze from the kitchen throughout the campground and drove Sammie crazy.

Mr. Yuni wore his blue Kung Fu jacket and Mrs. Cleerheart wove dragon blossoms through her long hair.

Sammie gathered bunches of wildflowers and placed them all around the graduation platform. She sneaked into the kitchen every few minutes to see if the yummy smelling food was done.

Molly assembled a big bouquet of fire lilies and arranged them in a tall vase next to Max's portrait gallery in the dining hall.

When the hour arrived, Max climbed on stage and called the dragons up one by one. He presented each of them with a special award to acknowledge their accomplishments.

Nate received a shiny Dragon Thermometer trophy to remind him of how he had mastered his hot temper. Molly's award was a glass figure in the shape of a fire lily. In tiny, gold leaf letters it read, A True Artist.

Sammie received a special pendant: a woodcarving created by her friend, Nate, in the shape of a paw. On the five toes were the letters P|A|U|S|E.

Phil's prize was a bunch of pencils and a stack of parchment. Max figured that Phil was not really the trophy type. But he sure went through a lot of paper.

Phil was thrilled.

When Raif's turn came, Max reached behind his own head, lifted his Dragon Tags up over his horns, and hung them around Raif's neck.

Raif stared in shock.

"Yay, Raif!" Sammie shouted. They all cheered.

Raif sat down and flipped through the tags. He read the messages engraved on the back of each one. See through the fault to the need...

Hmm.

After the dragons received their awards, Phil climbed up on stage and read his story. He was nervous at first, but as soon as he got past page one, he was in the zone, excited to share it.

The story was about them.

Everyone recognized Phil's fond, funny caricatures: Sammie's wild ways, Raif's bad boy facade, Max's insecurities. Phil spoofed Mr. Yuni and Mrs. Cleerhart as a fire-breathing drill sergeant and a hippie mother hen.

The group laughed and laughed till tears ran down their scales.

"Thank you, Phil." Mrs. C hugged him. He strolled back to his chair, happy with his first reading.

"Mr. Yuni, would you please come up and join me. We have one more award to present."

Mr. Yuni hobbled with his cane and hopped on stage. "As you all know, we had a new counselor this summer, and he turned out to be one of the best in the history of Dragon Camp."

The dragons erupted with applause.

"I'd like Raif to come up now and present this special award from all of us who so appreciate Max's dedication and talent."

They all hooted and whistled. "Yay, Max!" Sammie and Nate made gorilla sounds.

Max blushed and slowly approached the podium.

Raif carried a wooden crate like a nervous father holds a

newborn. Mrs. C lifted a colorful clay sculpture out of its container and placed it in Raif's arms.

Raif cleared his throat. "Coach Max..." He started to choke up. Geez! What is wrong with me? I'm turning into a big sissy.

He started again, determined to hide his feelings. "Coach Max, we learned a lot from you this summer. You were patient, and you worked hard to help us. No matter what, you were always there."

Max listened in disbelief. There must be some mistake. Raif was describing someone else.

"Before I walked up here, I was reading your Dragon Tags. One of them says, See through the fault to the need. That was you, Max, every day. You kept coming back and never let us push you away."

Max swallowed the lump in his throat.

"You showed us the kind of dragon we would like to be."

Max teared up against his will.

"So here is your prize. From your very first pack of dragons. We will never forget you."

Raif handed the sculpture to Max, who set it down on the podium to get a closer look.

A large green dragon created a semicircle with his outstretched wings. His massive embrace corralled and protected a small pack of colorful dragons: an orange girl, a purple boy, a pink girl, a blue boy, and a purple young adult dragon wearing boxing gloves.

Max smiled.

The little orange dragon held up a sign that said, We love you, Max! From your dragon pack.

When the ceremony was over, no one wanted to leave. It felt like sacred ground. The group talked and talked until they ran out of things to talk about.

"I'm bored," Sammie complained. "What's for lunch?"

"Wait a minute," Nate said. "What about Raif's surprise?"

"Yeah!" Sammie shouted. "Where's the surprise?"

Raif looked around at the faces of the eager dragons. Then he looked at Mr. Yuni and considered the consequences of what he was about to do.

He took a deep breath. What the heck. We live once.

"So, you're bored already." Raif grinned at Sammie.

"Yeah, too much talking. Not enough action."

"Would a piggyback ride cheer you up?"

"Yeah!" Sammie loved piggyback rides. Especially Raif's.

"Okay, hop on."

She climbed onto his back. "Hey, what about the surprise?"

"You'll see." Raif took off running toward the woods. Sammie bounced and giggled.

"Okay, squirt. Hold on tight. Here's your surprise." Raif extended his giant purple wings and launched up over the trees.

The group gasped.

Sammie squealed and clutched his neck. "Wow!"

He flew above the waterfall, down past the rapids, and back over the treetops to circle above Dragon Camp.

All eyes were fixed on the sky.

"Whoa!" Nate shouted. He stood staring with his mouth hanging open.

Molly sidled up to Phil and linked her arm through his. He blushed.

Sammie waved at her friends. "I can fly!"

Raif glided in and landed on the soft sand by the lake.

Sammie hopped off and ran to Max. "Did you see that? That was amazing!"

Max chuckled. "That Raif sure is full of surprises."

Mr. Yuni shook his head. What have I gotten myself into?

He gave Raif a playful look. "Is there an age limit on your piggy back rides?"

Raif's eyebrow scales popped up. "Seriously?"

"When you're my age, it's now or never."

Raif looked nervous as he knelt to help Mr. Yuni climb onto his strong back.

Mr. Yuni struggled and grunted. Then he flung his cane to the ground and clamped onto the scaly dragon's neck.

Raif looked back at his teacher. "Are you ready?"

"Ready as I'll ever be."

Raif's new friends shouted and cheered as he soared above the treetops with Mr. Yuni on his back.

Mrs. C laughed and let out a loud war whoop.

Mr. Yuni relaxed with a huge, satisfied smile. He could do this all day. "Hey, Raif. I've always wanted to see what's beyond the river."

Raif lit up. "Oh, you're going to like this." He surfed a strong tailwind, picked up speed, and soared high above the waterfall, beyond the forest, and over the breathtaking green mountains of a dragon frontier just waiting to be explored.

The End

Made in the USA
Coppell, TX
26 June 2024

33977243R00095